For Mom and Dad

EJ ALTBACKER

SCHOLASTIC INC.
New York Toronto London Auckland
Sydney Mexico City New Delhi Hong Kong

ISBN 978-0-545-43642-7

12 11 10 9 8 7 6 5 4 3 2 1   11 12 13 14 15 16/0

Printed in the U.S.A.   40

First Scholastic printing, December 2011

PROLOGUE

FOR TIME BEYOND MEMORY THERE WAS THE ocean and it was empty. Then the first fish, a shark named Tyro, was borne from it. Tyro circled the Big Blue's vastness and found he was alone. So he swam once more through the seven seas and with each stroke of his mighty tail created everything that lives in and under the waters. He chose several sharks to hunt with him and called these the First Shiver, positioning them in a Line from first to fifth, with himself as leader.

First was mighty Finnbarr whose descendants became the great white sharks; second was powerful Longfluke whose children became the bull sharks; third was the cunning Machiakelpi whose sons and daughters became the mako; Ramtail the Battler was fourth and his young became the tiger sharks; and fifth, but never considered last in the Line by Tyro, was Leynar the Magnificent, whose descendants would be the threshers.

First Shiver governed with one goal in mind: to protect its members, which numbered all of sharkkind, and to ensure their survival from one generation to the next. For many years, every shark and dweller living in the Big Blue prospered under shiver law.

But after a long life Tyro grew weary. He summoned his Five in the Line and told them that one day a great evil would threaten all of sharkkind and every dweller in the seven seas. When this day came, only a united First Shiver would be strong enough to defeat the evil. After this warning, Tyro gave himself to the Sparkle Blue, where his spirit swims the eternal current to this day. But after their leader was gone, those in the Line bickered and fought about who would be best to lead against the coming danger. In the end, the five sharks of First Shiver could not—and would not—agree, and so swam off by themselves to create their own shivers...

CHAPTER 1

SUNLIGHT DAPPLED THE WARM WATER AS GRAY flexed his powerful fins, gliding to a stop in a thick kelp bed. He used to hide in this patch of green-greenie unseen when he was smaller, but now his tail poked out. Gray made sure it waved back and forth with the warm tide so it wouldn't give him away. He would have been spotted going to the shiver's main hunting grounds, so he had snuck away in the opposite direction toward the lagoon. Gray was a growing fish, but the council, and his mom, Sandy, wouldn't let him hunt unsupervised. That was just unfair. He was twelve years old! He was practically adult for any sharkkind. Almost, anyway.

Even though his name was Gray, he was more bluish on his upper half and white on the bottom, with what he thought was a really cool stripe down each of his enormous flanks. "Everyone's jealous," he muttered. Apparently Gray was big for a reef shark. And ever since he grew larger than Atlas, the old bull shark who was Coral Shiver's leader, every fin watched him with a mixture of curiosity and fear. Like I'm a freak or something, he thought.

Gray pushed that from his mind and concentrated on the task at hand. He'd get into trouble for sure if the council, or his mom, found out he was this far away from the homewaters. And so near the lagoon, Gray thought. But this is where the tasty, tasty lobsters hang out. He gnashed his rows of razor-sharp teeth, imagining the satisfying crunch of a nice, plump shellhead. The lobster that Gray was hunting wandered into the next kelp bed over, which was even thicker than where Gray was hiding now, but no problem. Many sharkkind didn't like swimming through greenie because they were afraid they would get tangled. But not Gray. He swam where he wanted, when he wanted. And today that happened to be in a kelp bed. Now where was that lobster? Being such a great hunter, Gray was positive the dumb shellhead didn't have a clue that certain doom was coming for it.

But suddenly his prey jetted forward, abandoning all stealth and gaining speed. The lobster somehow sensed his presence and made a break for the lagoon where Gray couldn't swim safely anymore, not since his growth spurt. This was a little annoying. Gray used the currents to mask his stalking to perfection! Or not . . . How did this little krillface know he was watching? The lobster whizzed toward the mouth of the lagoon, where the landsharks had built some sort of floating home. Gray's mom would be really angry if she found out he was this close to the lagoon. But he wasn't about to be seen by anyone except the lobster. "And ol' Lobby will keep my secret once he's safely in my belly," Gray said out loud as he gained speed.

"Watcha doing, Gray?" asked Barkley the dogfish, disrupting Gray's concentration and even startling him a bit. Just a bit, though.

"Can't you see I'm busy?" Barkley could be very annoying. But still, he was Gray's friend and one of the few fish that made him laugh. He was also one of the few reef mates that would still spend time with Gray after his enormous growth spurt the previous year. Most of his old friends got very jumpy when he was around. Gray wondered why that was for a moment, but then set about leaving Barkley in his wake.

"Trying to catch that lobster, huh? Listen to your older and wiser friend—this isn't a good idea." Barkley was born a month before Gray and brought that fact up whenever he could.

"I'm not taking a survey about what you think!" Gray groused.

"Hey, I just don't want to see you with your head stuck in a bucket again." The dogfish grinned, now swimming upside down and eye to eye with Gray. The memory still stung.

When Gray was a pup, he explored an ancient wreck of a landshark boat, a galleon, and got his head stuck in a *bucket* which was something humans used to carry stuff around in. It had been wedged on so tight Prime Minister Shocks needed to ask three of the octos from the octopus clan to pull the thing off. Gray was called "bucket head" that entire summer. He pretended not to hear Barkley's teasing and increased his speed, but his friend was annoyingly fast for a dogfish and kept pace.

"Seriously, Gray, Miss Lamprey hunts around here before class. If she sees you, she'll tell your mom for sure," Barkley warned.

Everyone who grew up near the reef was taught by Miss Lamprey. They learned not only about the world in which they lived, but also about the dry world above the water where the two-legged landsharks ruled. Gray thought learning about the *human* world—that's what they called themselves—was a big waste of time. But it did make things easier if you knew the words for things that didn't come from the Big Blue. Especially if you got your head stuck in a bucket.

"Miss Lamprey can keep her pointy snout out of my business. And I thought we agreed to never bring up the *incident* again!"

"Oh, riiight. Totally forgot. Sorry. Let's head back to the reef," Barkley said as he tried to turn Gray by pressing against him. Ha! Fat chance. That used to work, but now Gray was four times the size of the dogfish who nonetheless strained against his bulk. "Seriously, stop being such a flipper! We're going to be late for class!"

"I am *not* a flipper!" Gray told the dogfish. "I'm a total fin!" Being a fin was very cool. Being a flipper wasn't.

"Well, you're not acting very finny!" Barkley said. Gray butted his friend to the side and sped forward. "Hey! Come back!" shouted the dogfish.

"Eat wake, buddy!" The lobster had passed into the mouth of the lagoon. Talking with Barkley cost Gray valuable time. But it still wouldn't be enough time for his prey to make it home. Gray would show the shellhead who was the big fish in this patch of water.

He bore down on the lobster. Gray could feel the warm water whisking through his gills and closed his mouth so it wouldn't slow him down. He could smell the lobster as he closed the distance between them. So delicious! He ground his teeth in anticipation. Closer. The lobster disappeared momentarily into the fronds of kelp near the opening of the lagoon. There wasn't enough to hide in, though. Gray sped through the sparse greenie, opening his mouth for his strike when—whammo!

But it wasn't a good whammo. Not good at all. Gray had hit a hidden shelf in the lagoon bed. He could feel his dorsal fin in the exposed air *above* the waterline! The lobster turned and clacked its claws at Gray while shimmying and flipping its tail back and forth. Was the shellhead doing some sort of victory swim?! Impossible!

Crustaceans were just dumb snacks. It sure seemed to be enjoying itself, though.

Barkley cruised to a stop, hovering near Gray. "Wow, that looked painful. And dumb! Was it more painful than dumb, you think? Or the other way 'round?"

Gray struggled, thrashing his tail to free himself. But he was stuck. "If you're finished, I could use some help!"

"Fine, fine." Barkley quickly swam to the shallower side of the lagoon and pushed. This accomplished nothing. He swam a tight circle and tried butting Gray off the shelf. "You know, you might want to lay off the fatty tuna and go on a seaweed diet for a while. I've heard it's very cleansing."

"Shut your cod hole and push!" Gray yelled. They were far too close to the landshark colony. And humans had things called boats to move on top of the Big Blue. One time Gray came upon a human in a rubber covering floating by the bottom of the reef. He was chasing a group of mackerel and didn't notice the human until they were snout to snout. It carried a spine shooter, and sometimes those were dangerous, even to a shark as big as Gray. But the landshark dropped it and blew bubbles instead, waving its arms wildly, looking very fierce indeed! It scared Gray so much he swam away as fast as he could! Close call. But this was more dangerous. Fish of all sizes—even whales!—were caught and killed by humans from boats.

Gray thrashed even harder. With one final ram from Barkley at full speed, he felt the ledge crumble, then disappear. He was free! Gray rejoiced as his dorsal fin submerged and he angled for deeper water.

"That was a close one, buddy!" Barkley chuckled nervously. After a moment, Gray did too. Pretty soon they were both cackling like crazy fish. "Can you imagine what your mom would do if she found out?" Barkley trailed off. Gray was laughing so hard he didn't notice his mother floating off to the side, her eyes blazing. Uh-oh.

"I think I'm going to find out," Gray said to his friend.

But Barkley wasn't there, of course. The dogfish had wisely vanished. How does he do that? Gray wondered silently as his mother frowned, her tail swishing in short, angry strokes.

CHAPTER 2

"YOU'RE GROUNDED FOR A WEEK!" HIS MOTHER said in a clipped voice, the barbels below her nostrils vibrating with emotion. They did that when she got mad. And she was angrier than Gray had seen her in a long while. Even madder than the time when he had talked Barkley into cutting school and got stung by a jellyfish. But seven days and nights of not swimming more than a body length away from the reef bed? Ridiculous! Was he some newborn pup that needed to hide in the greenie? No! Was he a bottom-feeding muck sucker that rooted in the sand for its meals? Disgusting! And again, no! Being grounded was no way for a big fin like him to spend even one day, much less a week!

But Gray's mouth was quicker than his brain so none of these perfectly good arguments made it into the conversation. Instead he blurted, "Awww, Mommm!"

"You broke your word to me," she said in a quiet voice.

"I'm sorry," he whispered.

Gray felt awful. Everyone in Coral Shiver respected his mother, proven by the fact that she had been chosen to be third in the Line. Gray was proud of that. Knowing how dangerous the Big Blue was, any shark in the Line could be your next leader. Usually shivers ranked five after their leader. It was an honor even though their shiver was small and didn't even have succession to the fifth, like a real battle shiver, only to the third.

Atlas was leader, of course. Then there was Quickeyes the thresher as his first and Onyx the blacktip as second. Onyx had these awesome markings down his flanks, almost like they were put there on purpose. But how? When Gray asked about the markings he got yelled at by both Onyx and his mom so he never asked again.

In a shiver, any shark could challenge for position, even for leader. But if you didn't have experience in the Line, you wouldn't be accepted as a contender by the full-member shiver sharks.

Since he was still technically a pup, Gray wasn't even a full member of Coral Shiver yet. "You have to earn the Line's respect before you can join as a shiver shark," his mother had told him when he was younger. Well, he hadn't earned any today.

"I know it's wrong to go toward the lagoon, but when I saw the lobster, I got so hungry!" Gray told her.

His mother sighed. "You're a growing shark, Gray. No one says you shouldn't eat." She looked him over from head to tail. He was now almost twice her length. "You just have to be smart about it. You have to do what's best for everyone, not just yourself. Even if that means you go hungry for a little while."

"I'm sorry," said Gray once again.

They entered the ancient lava vent, which was the entrance to the hidden reef and their homewaters. Landsharks lived in a floating base by the other reef, nearer to their shore. Ours is much nicer, thought Gray as he followed his mom's swishing tail down the secret path through the giant kelp bed. There was green-greenie, blue-greenie, and even yellow and brown-greenie. The greenie was long enough that it looked like just another giant seaweed bed from above. And if you didn't know where the path began while swimming in, you'd most likely get lost or hung up. Even landsharks stayed away because their boats got snared by the greenie that floated all the way up to the chop-chop. Crabs used their sharp claws to clip and trim the secret lane of the tangly plant. Supposedly. Gray had never actually seen them do it and didn't really believe shellheads were smart enough to follow instructions like that.

"Gray, the Coral Shiver homewaters are a special place," Sandy told him.

"I know that, Mom. I do live here."

Sandy let out an exasperated sigh. "That's not what

I mean. What we have here is different than many parts of the Big Blue."

Gray got excited. She was talking about the Big Blue in the way that meant open ocean! Would she let him go to the Tuna Run this year? He wasn't allowed last time because he was too young. They *had* to let him go this season! He couldn't help himself, and asked, "Can I go with you into the Big Blue for the Tuna Run? To see how it's different?"

"Absolutely not!" she said so sharply that Gray darted into the thick kelp. When he poked his head out, his mom sighed. She motioned for him to come out from the weedy bed. "I'm sorry I yelled. The open waters of the Big Blue are amazing and wonderful in places. But they can also be dangerous. Sharkkind and dwellers that make their home there aren't as nice as the ones here."

"Okay, Mom," Gray answered. "I'm not planning any trips away from the reef. I promise."

"You won't because you're grounded. And Barkley—come out here!"

Gray turned and saw Barkley hiding in the greenie. His eyes popped open as Sandy stared right at him. He nudged himself forward, smiling nervously. "Oh, here's the path! Silly me, I got lost. Hello, Miss Sandy."

Her eyes narrowed on the dogfish. "Hello to you, Barkley. Now, both of you get to class." And with a whisk of her tail she was gone.

"Grounded a whole week. Bummer," remarked the dogfish matter-of-factly. "By the way . . . told you so."

"By the way," Gray answered, "quit being a flipper."

Barkley led them around the main area of the reef. Most days at least one or two of the groups representing the different types of reef dwellers would meet about something or other. Anemones, starfish, sea cucumbers, jellies, tropicals, even shellheads, would speak with each other. Gray didn't know why. It wasn't as if they were smart like sharkkind. Most dwellers, or non-sharks, never spoke to sharkkind in general except when something important happened.

Even so, Prime Minister Shocks set the schedule so there wouldn't be what he called "unpleasantness" between groups that might make a meal out of each other. A group of urchins was talking with a cluster of brightly colored tangs. Gray knew these different groups each had their own hierarchy, even the shellheads supposedly, but didn't believe they could have anything interesting or important to say. They were colorful, though. He'd give them that.

Gray loved the riot of colors in the reef. Between the dwellers, algae, greenie, corals, mollusks, and plants, it was like an undersea rainbow. He saw a rainbow in the sky once, and it was a pale imitation of the undersea world. And at night the reef glowed even more spectacularly in places where the lumos gave off their pretty lights.

"Oh, I see a spot! Follow me!" said Barkley as he swam forward to claim an area near the front of the class and close to Miss Lamprey.

"What a sucker fish," muttered Gray. The dogfish heard and glared.

Miss Lamprey held class in different areas around the reef depending on what was being taught that day. Gray settled in, getting a few irritated looks from groups of angel and parrot fish whose view he accidentally blocked. One particularly annoying parrot fish went right through his mouth and yelled "Move it, wide load!" He almost told the parrot fish he wasn't fat, just big cartilaged, but he knew Miss Lamprey would make him repeat everything to the entire class if she heard. The fish swam around his eyes to be annoying before finding a new place a tail length away. Gray swallowed the urge to put the fish in its place by eating it. He was hungry again. Lately, Gray was always hungry. But he definitely didn't want to get into more trouble by eating a reef dweller.

His mother raised him to never harm anything that lived on or around this particular reef, just as every reef dweller did. There were exceptions, of course. The bottom feeders had their own disgusting ways of eating anything and everything, but sharkkind kept to a higher standard.

"It's not what we do here, Gray," she told him from his earliest days. "If a fish has color, find another. Silver or brown, gulp it down." That's what he learned when he was a pup. Or, even more of a pup than he was now. There was a difference between dumb fish that grouped together and mindlessly swam around (those you could eat) and the smarter ones who could hold a conversation (those you weren't supposed to eat). That's not to say any shark, being big or tough enough, couldn't eat whatever he or she wanted. But the decisions you made spoke to what type of citizen of the Big Blue you were. His mother said that sharkkind who chose to hunt intelligent ocean dwellers were more than bad sharks; they were evil. Gray thought it was worth the wait to find a cluster of dumb fish anyhow. There were always more of them!

Besides, breaking the rules carried consequences. One of Barkley's cousins, Hegger, ate a scarlet grouper when he and Barkley were little. Despite the name, a colored grouper was not a mindless, grouping fish. And this particular scarlet grouper lived on the reef. Anyway, Hegger was *accidentally* stung by an urchin the next day and almost died. Hegger swore it was a payback and he was probably right. Urchins were low down, poisonous sneaks who did that sort of thing.

The lesson in Miss Lamprey's class today was about current and drift in the open waters of the Big Blue. Gray barely listened. When was he ever going to experience that? Never. Gray allowed himself to float upward a bit to stretch his flippers.

"Umm, Gray?" whispered Barkley. Gray looked over

at the dogfish who smugly reminded him, "You're grounded, remember?" Technically he wasn't a body length from the reef bottom.

Gray grimaced and lowered himself. "Thanks, buddy. Who would have thought you could be so helpful with your snout so far up Miss Lamp—"

"Gray!" yelled Miss Lamprey, cutting him off. "Would you please stop bothering Barkley and pay attention?"

"Sorry, Miss Lamprey." Gray settled almost on the seabed. He sighed and couldn't wait for moonrise. This day was a total bust.

CHAPTER 3

THE CARIBBI SEA WHERE THE CORAL SHIVER reef lay was clear and calm when the moon rose. After class Gray and Barkley went swimming. At least, in the areas where Gray was allowed after his punishment. Tonight everyone was getting along, however, which made them exceedingly dull to watch.

"You want to see if those crabs are still fighting?" Barkley asked.

"Who wants to watch a couple of shellheads whacking and clacking over some snail carcass? Gross!" They swam in silence but in the general direction of the feisty crabs, there being nothing better to do. "I'd give anything to be out in the open waters with cold water rushing down my flanks. I'm the type of fin that needs action and adventure!" Gray told his friend. "But where do I live? The quietest reef in the entire *history* of the Big Blue, that's where!"

"Well it's about to get a lot less quiet." Barkley pointed his snout in the direction of a sea dragon whom everyone around the homewaters had nicknamed "Yappy." Gray didn't even know his real name. "I hope you're happy," the dogfish muttered. "You jinxed us."

Most dwellers wouldn't talk to others not of their kind unless they had some sort of business, or knew them well, or it was an emergency. But Yappy talked with *anyone* he came across, no matter if they wanted to or not. One time everyone thought that ancient Janprickle the urchin had died. Yappy started talking to her and wouldn't stop for an entire day. Nonstop. In a crazy way, it was kind of impressive. Just as Janprickle's fellow urchins were going to *honor* the old dweller in their way by eating her—yuck—she shook herself a couple times and joined the conversation. Janprickle and Yappy talked for another whole day! Not only could Yappy talk you to death, apparently he could talk you *out* of death, too.

And for some reason Yappy thought Barkley and Gray were his best buddies, so it was extra inconvenient for them to bump into him. Even in the weak moonlight, Yappy's bright yellow body made him stand out. He also had blue stripes along his belly and orange highlights on the tips of his weedy flippers and tail. These were supposed to help him blend into the greenie when hunting small crabs and shrimp. But between the nonstop talking and his very bright coloring, it was hard to imagine Yappy blending in anywhere.

"Keep swimming. Don't make eye contact," whispered Gray.

Barkley agreed wholeheartedly. "Nod and gnash your teeth like we're talking about something serious and maybe—"

"Hey fellas! Isn't the moon just gilly tonight? You ever wonder what the moon is made of?"

"Yappy—" Barkley attempted to get a word in edgewise.

"I heard if a marlin jumps at just the right angle when there's a full moon, he can spear it with his nose. Do you think marlins eat bits of the moon for fifteen nights, and it grows back the other fifteen?"

Barkley tried again, "Yap—"

"If they *are* eating the moon and not sharing, I say the council should get involved. I mean, who do those selfish, moon-eating morons think they are anyway?"

"YAPPY!" shouted Gray, blowing the much smaller sea dragon back a fluke length. This got his attention.

"Yes, Gray?"

"Barkley and I would love to hear your theories on marlins eating the moon, but we're doing some, umm, serious talking about . . . things." Gray glanced at his friend to jump in anytime.

Barkley was never slow on the uptake. "That's right. Important shiver business. Sorry, we can't tell you about it. Or we could, but then we'd totally have to eat you."

"I get it. My cousins in the Dark Blue are always up to super secret stuff about prophecies that could mean the end of the entire Big Blue as we know it! I can't tell you about that, either. Did you know my cousins are giants? Bigger than Gray even! They would just eat that drove of bluefin right up, I tell ya!" Yappy said as he rocked back and forth with the tide.

"Excellent!" Barkley chimed as the sea dragon opened his mouth to say something else. "Let's agree to keep our various secrets safe and swim away without any more talking, so we don't accidentally doom the seven seas." Barkley tried to shove Gray forward.

"Wait, what did you mean by 'drove of bluefin'?" asked Gray, suddenly very interested.

"You guys didn't know? The angelfish are sooo miffed. A double drove of bluefin totally stole a swarm of shrimp from them." Yappy pointed toward the far end of the reef with a back fin. "Never heard such foul language from an angel in my life! Shocking, really."

Gray fairly vibrated with excitement. A double drove of delicious bluefin was swimming around and distracted by shrimp? Near the reef? His stomach rumbled. That was two hundred fish at least.

Sharks counted fish groupings by cluster, drove, horde, shimmer, shoal, legion, and siege. Clusters were tens, droves were hundreds, a horde was in the thousands, shimmers were ten thousands, a shoal was one hundred to four hundred thousand, legions numbered at five hundred to nine hundred thousand, and a siege was over a *million* fish.

Gray had never seen anything larger than a lower shoal, and those were teeny-tiny krill. They really didn't count unless you could fill up on those ugly, shrimpy things. The older sharks in the shiver said that in the times of their fathers and their father's fathers the Tuna Run was every sixth moon and was always a double or triple siege. Gray couldn't even picture what two or three million fish might look like. And supposedly, a siege of bluefin was so fast and dense it could injure or even kill a shark. Gray was sure they were yanking his tail, though. How could a bunch of fish do that to a shark? Only by overeating, he thought, which was a chance Gray was willing to take if he got lucky enough to see a siege. If he ever even made it to a Tuna Run. But maybe he could have his own little Tuna Run right now!

"I do not like that look," Barkley said as he watched the smiling Gray. "Not at all."

"Let's go fishing!" Gray rocketed under and around several brightly colored coral pillars, scaring the heck out of the crabs, eels, and other dwellers trying to stealthily hunt on them.

Barkley struggled to keep up, panting. "Wait, stop!" Just then Gray did stop, reversing himself so fast the dogfish plowed into his tail fin. Barkley let out an "Ooof!"

"Quiet!" Gray told the dogfish. "Look."

There they were: hundreds and hundreds of big, fat bluefin there for the taking!

CHAPTER 4

"GRAY, THAT'S INTO THE OPEN OCEAN FOR SURE," Barkley said. "And you're grounded!"

"Oh, come on! That's still Coral Shiver homewaters." Gray nodded to himself, salivating. "And dumb fish are always fair game! Why, we could get in trouble for *not* eating them!"

Barkley smiled sarcastically. "I know the rules on what to eat and when to eat it better than you, megamouth." The dogfish tapped him on the belly with his tail. "By the way, have you gained weight since this morning?"

"Hey, I'm big cartilaged!" Gray said indignantly. "And if you're done insulting me ..." He waggled a fluke at the fish.

"Fine, Overbiter is on duty for shiver business. Let's tell him about the drove. We'll be heroes!" Barkley swished his tail happily at the thought.

Gray snorted. "Please! Overbiter is like a hundred and sleeps all the time. He can't swim fast enough to catch these blues. You don't want to make him look bad in front of everyone, do you?"

Maybe embarrassing Overbiter wasn't Gray's main worry, but the lemon shark *was* half senile. By the time they explained everything to him, the bluefin would be long gone. Barkley hesitated as he glanced longingly at the tuna feeding on the swarm of shrimp. "I'd hate to embarrass him, I guess."

Barkley drooled a little and Gray knew he had him. "Let's get our fill, and then go tell everyone. We'll still be heroes!"

The dogfish flicked his fins up and down in agreement and flashed forward so suddenly it momentarily surprised Gray. He did not just do that! Gray sped up, overtaking his friend. He aimed for a plump bluefin but never got there. Two others accidentally swam into his open mouth just before he was going to strike, along with a load of shrimp! It caught Gray by surprise and he gagged. This would be a story told around the glowing algae pylons for years to come—Gray the big, bad reef shark chokes to death on dinner! An extremely large blue slammed into his throat, kicking in a reflexive swallow. I really should remember that spot on my throat, he thought to himself. But later! The combo of bluefin and shrimp was scrumptious!

Gray and Barkley laughed and ate. It was crazy! No sooner were they done with one fish than they each caught another. The pair tried to keep count of who caught the most but gave up; the bluefin were eaten so fast and furiously. Then, as all groupings did, the fish thinned and disappeared. Pretty soon only a couple of woozy shrimp were all that was left. Barkley listed to the side. "Ohh, I think I might have eaten too much. By the way, where are we?"

Good question. How long had they been feeding? Gray wasn't sure. The reef wasn't in sight anymore. In fact, nothing around them looked familiar. Gray couldn't even see the bottom. They were definitely off the reef and into the open waters of the Big Blue now. They would get into serious trouble if someone found out.

Gray was about to say something when he felt a prickle of electricity go up his spine, a fin flick before a gray-and-white blur screamed into view. This alarm system saved Gray's life at least twice when he was younger, once when a huge moray eel hiding in a crevice surprised him. It was a vague buzzing that set him on edge right before danger struck. He now knew it was a survival instinct, but Gray hadn't felt it for a long time, not since his growth spurt.

Just in time, with a stroke of his powerful tail, he was able to deflect a shark's headlong attack at his dorsal fin. It was a tiger shark and he was massive! Larger than Gray was, even!

Barkley was indignant. "What's your damage, jelly-brain? We're trying to digest here!" He coasted in front of Gray protectively as the tiger carved a turn and rushed at them once more. It must have dawned on Barkley that being a motionless target wasn't the brightest idea because he dove underneath the gnashing jaws of the tiger. The big flipper only gave a halfhearted snap at the dogfish. He was plainly after Gray, since his size made him the main threat.

Well, he's got that right! Gray thought as he sped up. They were lost, probably in trouble, and now some flipper was trying to eat them! Enough was enough. Gray accelerated out of the tiger's way before slashing his own turn downward and underneath the attacking shark. The tiger lost sight of Gray for a moment and hesitated. It was all the time Gray needed.

"You lose," said Barkley from his hovering position above the momentarily confused tiger. Gray heard a satisfying "Whuufff!" as he rammed the shark in the soft underbelly by his liver. The tiger tried to turn but was momentarily paralyzed. Barkley hammered the dazed attacker next. Or he tried. Because of his small size, he bounced off like a sea horse against hard coral. Gray wouldn't let his advantage slip away, though. He bore down on the tiger, ready to rip a fin off with his razor teeth.

"Wait! Wait!" yelled the tiger. "I'm with Goblin Shiver, and you're dead meat if you touch me!"

Gray chose to ignore this, but had to come to an abrupt halt when Barkley swam right in front of his mouth! "What are you doing?"

"Saving our lives!" Barkley whispered before turning to the tiger. "Sorry for the misunderstanding!"

"Misunderstanding?" Gray sputtered. "He tried to eat us!"

The big shark recovered somewhat, and the chance to send him to the Sparkle Blue passed. Gray hoped Barkley knew what he was doing. The tiger wouldn't be easily beaten a second time.

"Listen to your friend," said the tiger. "This is Goblin Shiver territory. You don't have permission to hunt here unless Goblin, or maybe Gafin, give their say-so. And I know you don't know Goblin. So, do you know the urchin king?"

Gray understood little of what the big tiger was saying. "We need permission to hunt?" he asked, genuinely puzzled.

"Of course you do! I thought you were from Razor Shiver, poaching our feeding grounds," the tiger commented, watching Gray and Barkley for their reactions. "But I can see I was wrong. My name is Thrash, by the way."

"I'm Gray and this is Barkley."

"Where are you from?" the tiger named Thrash asked suspiciously.

"Coral Shiv—" Gray began, but Barkley cut him off immediately.

"A coral reef where we rested! But there were landsharks so we left. Now we're here. Nice to meet you!"

Thrash dismissed Barkley but swam around Gray, looking him over. "I thought you were a great white, but you're not. You're just a pup! Don't think I've seen a shark like you before. What are you, anyway?"

"I'm a reef shark," Gray answered proudly.

Thrash laughed. "Oh, that's good! Yeah, right, reef shark! Goblin loves a sense of humor. Sometimes." The tiger indicated the direction he wanted them to follow. "Come on, he's going to want to look you over."

Neither of them moved. "Look us over?" asked Barkley.

"To be a part of Goblin Shiver," answered Thrash. "We're at war with Razor Shiver and can always use another shark who knows how to fight. Whatever you are."

Barkley swam between the large tiger and Gray. "Actually, we're not real big joiners, Thrash. We're more rogue fish."

"Rogues swim alone," said Thrash with a hint of malice. "That's why they're rogues."

Barkley got flustered. "Sure, we know that, everyone knows that! We're a rogue *pair*. It's a new thing we invented. Again, nice meeting you. We'll be going now." The dogfish kept his voice low when he passed Gray. "Let's get out of here while the getting's good."

Gray followed, unsure why Barkley was acting so strangely but knowing deep down he didn't want to be involved with a maniac tiger shark that talked about wars and had almost eaten him a moment ago. "Yeah, rogue pair. That's us."

Thrash caught Gray's eye before he swam away. "You'll have to pick a side sooner or later, pup. Everyone will have to pick a side." With a chuckle and a dismissive flick of his tail, the tiger shark left.

"Let's go home," Barkley told Gray, who quietly followed his friend.

Their first trip into the open water had been a real eye opener, but not in a good way.

CHAPTER 5

"NO, NO, NO!" YELLED GOBLIN LOUD ENOUGH to attract attention all around his homewaters. He gnashed his teeth so hard he felt one break and saw it drift to the sandy bottom. A crab scuttled over and began probing the tooth to see if there was anything to eat inside it. It almost made Goblin laugh, but the situation was too serious to allow that right now. "We need to keep up *all* our patrols! Razor Shiver isn't going to rest and neither can we!"

"You're telling me what you want, and I'm trying to tell you what's possible," Ripper replied evenly. The big, battle-scarred hammerhead was close to insubordination. But then he ducked his head and added, "I suppose we could promote a couple of the pups into full shiver sharks to make up for—you know—"

Goblin took time to appear thoughtful. His mother, the shiver leader before him, had always told him to do this. "Good idea. Let them flex their fins a little. When I was a pup, I couldn't wait to get into the thick of things!"

It wasn't as if he was much older than a pup now, being just fifteen. For great whites, fifteen was physically mature. But some of the sharkkind that Ripper was thinking of were a little *too* young and weren't experienced enough to survive a real battle. They could be used for patrols and as an early warning system, though, which would free up his veterans for more important things. Not a perfect solution, but it would do for now.

Goblin stared imperiously at his Five in the Line. Ripper was his first, a giant hammerhead and the only shark who might be tougher than himself. Thrash, the tiger, was his second. Goblin's third was Streak, a blue shark who was small for her kind but made up for it in sheer ferocity. Churn was an oceanic whitetip and his fourth. Goblin had known Churn since the whitetip was a pup. Then there was his fifth: Velenka, a sleek, black mako.

Velenka was undoubtedly the smartest and most beautiful shark he ever met. Such big eyes. She could have been his fourth, maybe even third. She was invaluable as an adviser. Why the mako didn't make a move up the Line was puzzling to Goblin. Velenka hadn't even won her rank by combat, as was custom when a position in the Line opened. It was done by vote after Goblin's last fifth, Hawley, was found floating on the surface in the chop-chop three months ago. Hawley wasn't attacked by sharkkind; there were no bite marks. His corpse was grotesquely swollen as if he had died a week earlier. But Goblin swam with the thresher the night before he was found, so he knew that wasn't the case. He had trusted Hawley most of all, and the thresher worshipped Goblin like an older brother. It was a bitter loss, but that was life in the open waters of the Big Blue.

"What do you want to do, Goblin?" asked Velenka. The mako spoke more than any of the others even though she was only his fifth. It was a little odd, even presumptuous, but Velenka did keep things on point. The others waited for Goblin's answer.

"Can't you see I'm thinking?" He snapped at the mako, his bulk nudging hers out of hover. "Do you have a current you're late for? Someplace more interesting to go?"

"I didn't mean any disrespect," she answered.

"And that's why I'm not feeding on your carcass!" he yelled.

His shiver, now called Goblin Shiver instead of Riptide Shiver, had gotten their tails kicked by the bull sharks of Razor Shiver a day ago. They'd lost two soldiers and hadn't sent any bulls to the Sparkle Blue. Razor and his shiver controlled the best hunting grounds in the entire North Atlantis and also owned a prized territory for the Tuna Run. This annoyed Goblin. It was because of Razor naming his shiver after himself that Goblin had done the same. He would never admit that, of course. Razor Shiver weren't the only tough gang of sharkkind on the Western edge of the Atlantis, but they were the strongest today. Food was growing scarce, with fewer and fewer large groupings to feed on. Goblin and his shiver would stay near the muck-sucking bottom if he couldn't figure out a way to recruit more warriors and conquer new territory!

And to top things off, Thrash now swam in as though he was being chased by a prehistore nightmare with a story about a *pair* of rogue sharks named Gray and Barkley. And this Gray was a mysterious giant type of Sharkkind Thrash had never seen before! His Five in the Line and the rest of the full members of the shiver were looking at Goblin now, waiting for answers. His shiver sharks hovered listlessly behind the Line, speaking and joking in low voices with each other. At one time there would have been order, every mariner hovering in its own row, waiting for the leader's orders to be carried out by subcommanders. When Goblin was young, discipline and numbers were the mark of a true battle shiver. But now...

Everyone was always waiting for answers from him. It was what Goblin liked least about being leader. Sometimes he wished his mother were still around. She would know what to do, he thought to himself.

Goblin turned to Thrash. "You're sure they weren't just passing through? Maybe from the Sific Ocean?"

The tiger shook his head from side to side. "Nah, they mentioned a coral reef. I think they're from somewhere near shore. They were soft."

"Beat you, didn't they?" noted Ripper. Goblin saw that the tiger took the insult personally, but if Thrash got mad the big hammerhead could take care of himself. That's why he was Goblin's first.

"Who cares about a couple of yokels from the boonie-greenie who don't know anything about the Big Blue?" yelled Streak. The undersize blue was seething. "We lost Scrape and Jonquil to the bulls! Let's attack and even the score!"

Streak would want to fight no matter what because Scrape was her brother. But Goblin was pretty sure the blue didn't care one way or another that Jonquil was gone. He had just joined the shiver recently.

"Bad idea!" cried Churn. "We should take some time to regroup." The whitetip had almost been eaten by Razor himself in the battle and sported a ragged bite mark across the gills to show just how close he'd come to death. Churn was now one jumpy fin and would be for a while longer.

"Coward!" Streak yelled angrily. "Swim off the Line, useless! Go find a turtle shell to hide inside!"

Churn might be jumpy, but he was much bigger than Streak. Goblin was about to lose control as his third and fourth tried to eat each other! But then, the smell of an enemy interrupted the budding fight. Everyone looked over as a solitary bull swam close enough to be seen, but far enough away to retreat. Goblin's spine tingled with the sense of impending battle. He was about to charge the bull when Velenka spoke.

"I don't think he's here for trouble," she said.

"How would you know?" snarled Streak.

Velenka took no notice of the blue's tone but answered the question instead. "You know what an attack looks like better than anyone, Streak. What do you think?"

Streak calmed herself and watched the lone bull for a moment. "Okay, he's not on offense. But who is he and why's he here?"

"That's exactly what we should ask him." Velenka swam forward, drawing Goblin with her. "Maybe this has something to do with the two sharks Thrash saw?" The mako seemed happiest when she was puzzling something out. Or scheming. She once told Goblin that her hero was the legendary Machiakelpi, the mako who swam in the First Shiver and supposedly ruled the entire Sific after Tyro left for the Sparkle Blue. Goblin had to admit Velenka was a schemer worthy of Machiakelpi's reputation.

"Keep your place behind me, Fifth!" He took the lead. Maybe this shark was an opportunity. If it was, Goblin wanted the credit for leading. And it wasn't as though he would let Velenka meet the bull without him.

Velenka tried to keep her excitement in check but felt her spine tingling as they swam to meet Kilo. She knew that the bull would play his part and pretend they'd never met before. But could he play it well enough so that Goblin wouldn't sense something out of the ordinary? That was the question. That was why she needed to carefully control the conversation. Goblin might be dim, but he wasn't without instinct. You didn't stay shiver leader for long without good instincts.

And who was the mysterious giant Thrash had tussled with? No one else had noticed the large tooth lodged underneath the tiger's fin. Was it important? Its shape looked so familiar for some reason. Velenka had knocked the tooth free before anyone could see, and it floated into the darkness below. She didn't need Goblin distracted just now, not when she was setting her plan into action.

Velenka would send Thrash back in the direction the mysterious sharks came from to find their home. Perhaps Kilo and his bulls could be useful in this also. Always bend circumstance to your advantage. Machiakelpi taught that eons ago. Good advice, then and now.

"Maybe I should find out why this bull is here?" Velenka asked Goblin. "That way you can watch for lies when he speaks. Besides, why should this puny flipper talk to you, our shiver leader, as if he's your equal?"

Goblin nodded as they stopped a few body lengths from Kilo. "Good," he said quietly. "Do it."

Velenka smiled as she swam forward. There was destiny in the current! She could feel it!

CHAPTER 6

AFTER SWIMMING FOR THE REST OF THE NIGHT—the sun was rising by the time Gray and Barkley got back—they reached the reef. How had they gotten so far away?

The worst part was the place was in an uproar. Gray hoped in vain it wasn't because of them.

Of course he was very, very wrong.

Atlas led the Line, along with many other shiver sharks, in a ragged, three-level triangle formation. That was weird. Gray had never seen them do that. What did it mean? They certainly didn't look happy, though.

"Gray!" cried his mom. "Are you all right?" She tried to swim ahead of Atlas but was slowed by Quickeyes and Onyx.

Atlas gave her a hard look. "Sandy, please." Gray's mom nodded, and the Coral Shiver leader spoke again, "Gray, Barkley—are you okay?" Quickeyes and Onyx swam overhead, watching the distant waters. Why were they doing that?

"We are," answered Barkley. Gray quickly agreed with his friend.

"Now tell me exactly where you were, and anything that happened," Atlas ordered. Gray had never seen the old bull shark so . . . *commanding* before. Barkley told the story with Gray adding bits and pieces. Oddly, the more the story went on, the angrier Atlas and the others became. Except Gray's mom. She got scared.

A full council of all the reef dwellers was called. The sharks of Coral Shiver wanted to make the decision by themselves but were overruled by Prime Minister Shocks. Shocks would have probably let Atlas, Sandy, and the others in Line hand out Gray's punishment, but the other reef dwellers demanded their say.

Gray wasn't sure what was happening, exactly, but his mom was even more upset than yesterday. Quick-eyes and Onyx took turns staring at Gray as if they wanted to eat him. Overbiter was busy gnawing on his own tail fin. He used to be second in the Line years ago and sometimes didn't remember he wasn't a member of the council anymore. Atlas and the rest never said anything and let him stay. Supposedly he had been a great warrior long ago. Yeah, right.

Shocks sent a weak bolt of electricity arcing into the water, calling everyone in the area to attention. Gray had never seen so many dweller leaders gathered at one time! There were all kinds of fish; tangs, grouper, lantern fish, angelfish, hatchet fish, clown fish, puffers, wrasse, frog fish, sunfish, doctor, and surgeonfish. Every other non-fish dweller seemed to be here too: big and small rays, eels of all sizes and colors, anemones, urchins, shellheads, turtles, and many, many others.

This would be really neat if I wasn't the reason they were here, Gray thought as he floated above the flat stone that was traditionally known as Speakers Rock. It didn't seem like he would get to speak, but there was no good area for everyone to see him otherwise, so Atlas allowed it.

Barkley was asked questions by the manta rays, their pilot fish nearby. Some of these rays were wider than Gray, and their larger cousins, the giants, were bigger in all ways. Supposedly rays were distant cousins of sharkkind from prehistore times. He didn't really believe it as they weren't very good hunters, living mostly on floating greenie, krill, and shellheads. They did have really cool stingers, but didn't use them for hunting. What a waste!

Gray watched his mother become more and more agitated as Prime Minister Shocks spoke with her. Gray wished he could hear, but they were in a place where the currents masked their conversation. The other dwellers who could listen in seemed satisfied, though. Suddenly the current shifted, and Gray could hear parts of what his mom and Shocks were talking about.

"You know what's out there!" his mother said. "Battle shivers are on the move! The Indi King's armada—"

The tide shifted, and Gray could only hear Shock's reply in bits, "...are only rumors!"

Battle shivers? That was the kind of intensely interesting stuff Gray always wanted to hear about—the stuff adults whispered and then stopped discussing whenever he or Barkley got close. For a moment Gray thought his mother was going to bite the distinguished eel. Shocks spoke to the next group of dwellers, and pretty soon everyone *except* Gray knew what was happening.

Come on!

Atlas and the other sharkkind in the Line tried to calm his mom, but it wasn't working. Gray felt awful. Why do I keep disappointing her? She broke free and swam toward him. Prime Minster Shocks tried to get ahead of her, but she left the eel tumbling in her wake with a furious tail stroke. "That's totally out of order, Sandy!" he harrumphed.

"I want a minute with my son!" she yelled, close to tears, her barbels quivering. After a stare down, Shocks gave her a curt nod. She approached Gray and said, "Just tell the truth, okay? We'll get through this."

Get through what? he wondered. Gray was becoming irritated. A growing shark has to eat! They couldn't punish him for that. But a creeping feeling in his belly told him that they could.

Prime Minister Shocks let off another low-voltage attention grabber that quieted everyone. "Gray, please swim over here so everyone can listen to you answer my questions."

"Umm, sure." Gray moved to the area where the current would catch his words and broadcast them.

"Why did you leave the reef homewaters last night?" Shocks asked.

Everyone was listening and watching intently and Gray became nervous. "I, umm, I mean, we—" He looked over at Barkley. "We saw some fish and got hungry. They were mixed with shrimp, very delicious, by the way, and also—"

The gathered dwellers' whispering rose in volume as Shocks cut him off. "But wasn't it *you* who convinced your friend to go? In fact, didn't he say that you shouldn't leave the reef?"

"Well, yeah. But he's always trying to keep me from doing fun stuff—" Gray stopped in confusion as the murmurs from the dwellers got louder, in some cases surging to outright yelling. Except for his mother. She was crying now. Atlas glared again. Gray continued with his point, speaking over the crowd so he would be heard. "Hey, I was hungry!" For some reason this made things much worse.

Shocks zapped the water with a heavy charge to quiet the crowd enough so he could speak. "ORDER!" he yelled. "I will have order!" The eel turned to Gray.

"Is that why you left the reef and drew the attention of a tiger shark, who was himself a member of a shiver? Because you were hungry?"

"Umm, well, I didn't go out there with the intention of meeting anyone, but, yes, I was hungry."

"So you put your hunger ahead of the safety of everyone on the reef. Is that right? I hope you're at least full!"

It took a moment for Gray to realize what he was being asked. Unfortunately, his mouth was already speaking. "I'm still a little hungry but—wait—what?"

The gathered dwellers exploded, everyone shouting, clacking their claws, basically making any loud noise they could as a sign of their anger. Prime Minster Shocks futilely shot electrical charges into the water. He needed to call the rest of his eel friends to raise the voltage before he got everyone's attention and order was restored.

"Mom!" said Gray as she swam close to him. "I'm really sorry! I'm—"

She cut him off with a slash of her tail. "I know you are, Gray. Look, there's something I haven't told you. You're going to have a brother and a sister. "

"What?!"

His mother was much sadder than he would expect her to be as she told him the news. "You're going to be a big brother. Oh, Gray, I'm so sorry." She sobbed.

"Why are you sorry? Why are you crying?" he asked.

"This is great! I've always wanted brothers and sisters!" Then Gray grew confused. "I really am happy, but why are you telling me now? I don't exactly get it."

There were tears in his mother's eyes as she said, "Because that's the reason I can't go with you!"

"Go with me? Where?"

Sandy was led away by Atlas and the other sharks in the Coral Shiver Line. "Meet me at the Tuna Run! Prove yourself as a strong and good hunter and they'll take you back!" The noise grew so loud that Gray could no longer hear his mother.

The Tuna Run! He was allowed to go! But what did she mean by take him back?

He grew cold and afraid as Prime Minister Shocks swam near Speakers Rock directly in front of Gray. It was then he noticed that Barkley was also blubbering. This isn't going to be good, he thought.

Shocks cleared his throat to speak. There was absolute silence now. "Gray, you've endangered the shiver because of your own selfish desires. If this was the first time you needed to be disciplined it might be different. But it isn't, so . . . " Shocks looked at him sadly but pronounced the sentence in a clear voice. "You are hereby banished from Coral Shiver!"

INTO
THE
BIG
BLUE

CHAPTER 7

THE WORD ECHOED IN GRAY'S EARS LIKE THE TIDES.

Banished.

Prime Minister Shock's word was law by the reef, and even though Gray was a big fish, the sentence would be carried out. The octos from the octopus clan were waiting with their foul jets of black ink if he didn't obey. And the seedier bottom feeders who lived on the dark side of the reef—Orin the scorpion fish and his friends came to mind—were poisonous enough to send even Gray to the Sparkle Blue if he caused trouble. Aside from his mom and Barkley, Gray's only ally was Yappy! And that was only because Yappy's family couldn't *stop* him from talking. Not until they caught him, anyway.

For a moment Gray almost chuckled at the thought of Yappy zipping around, with so many others chasing him and yelling, "This is a slippery slope! What will you do when they come for you? Slippery slope! Slippery slope!" But Gray sobered quickly, remembering how Barkley's family ushered him away before he had the chance to react at all. That was probably a good thing. The dogfish could get emotional sometimes.

"At least I didn't give them the satisfaction of throwing me out," Gray muttered. He swam out, head high, on his own. Truthfully, the reef and Coral Shiver homewaters were too small for a fin like him. Gray needed space if he was going to live it up. Maybe Prime Minister Shocks had done him a big, fat favor.

It sure didn't really feel that way, though.

Gray almost began to sob but stopped when he saw a giant sea turtle staring as it leisurely floated by. "What you lookin' at, shellback? You want a piece of me?" The turtle churned its stubby legs a little faster. For their kind this was the equivalent of a panicked rush. Gray was satisfied with the reaction, so he didn't go ram the turtle. "You better not tell anyone I was crying!" he yelled at the turtle's receding figure. "Because I'm not!"

Gray had traveled for three entire days, near as he could figure. When he was near the reef, he could sense the depth of the water and didn't need to open his eyes to tell if it was day or night. In this open water, Gray stayed near the surface to keep himself oriented.

Not that he was afraid to go deeper, of course. He just didn't want to go deeper *right* now. "At least the sun shines into the water the same way," he said aloud. But it was colder and the current stronger. Not like home at all. What I'd give to be grounded by the reef again, he thought sadly.

Gray looked down to where the water darkened. Although he could sense the bottom was there, he couldn't see it. How did dwellers there even know what time it was? It was even colder than the water around him. And always black as night. Gray's stomach churned. He was hungry, but the ocean seemed absolutely empty! It was eerie. And when there were fish, they came and went so fast he actually missed with his strikes. Compared to the ones by the reef, these fish were bigger, stronger, and faster. Gray's stomach growled again, and he grew scared. Maybe he'd just starve in the open waters.

"Hey, Gray!" Gray almost jumped out of his skin. It was Barkley!

"Would you stop doing that?" Gray sputtered, momentarily forgetting his situation. But *only* for a moment. They were a very long distance from the reef. "What are you doing here?"

Barkley was uncharacteristically tongue-tied for a moment. "Umm, nothing. Just stretching the ol' fins. You know me, always trying to broaden my horizons."

"Go home."

Barkley made a rude noise. "Who do you think you are, ordering me around? Takiza the magical fighting fish?"

Gray chuckled despite the situation. Takiza was a legendary fish who supposedly could conjure whirlpools and underwater lightning with magic. There were lots of fantastic stories about Takiza, who went by lots of different names depending on whom you asked. One time he supposedly fought ten great whites, the meanest of all sharkkind, and beat them easily when they threatened a baby dolphin. It was a fantastic tale and obviously just for amusement. "Be a good shark or Takiza will come and put you in your place!" The worst part of it was that Barkley's dumb comment reminded him of the reef and his mom telling him stories about Takiza, which made him even more homesick.

Gray sighed. Even though he was arguing with Barkley, the truth was that he *wanted* his friend to stay. But that was wrong. Gray was exiled and Barkley wasn't. His home was by the reef, and Gray couldn't let him throw that away. "I know what you're doing, but you should turn around."

"And I know what you're doing, Gray. But we've been friends since you were born—I was born first, so of course I remember—and I *want* to come along. I was going to sign up for Miss Lamprey's migration class this year, anyway. This'll be like that, only better! Besides, you think I'm going to let you hoard all the adventure like some adventure-hoarding hermit crab?"

Gray replied with a subdued "Okay, then." It was all he could do not to burst into tears. Tough fin you are, he thought to himself.

They found a swift current, which pulled them deeper and deeper into the open waters of the Big Blue. Gray enjoyed the silence for a time. But with Barkley being Barkley, silence never lasted too long.

"So, where we going?"

"Umm, into the open ocean," Gray answered with as much confidence as he could muster.

Barkley sighed. "Yes, I'm aware of that—being here and all. We're into the Atlantis Ocean now, North Atlantis, by the way. But where do you want to end up?"

"I don't know. I started swimming in this direction after they kicked me out. I didn't have some big exile plan ready to go. You know, you can get annoying in a fin flick!" But Gray wasn't really mad at Barkley. He was mad at himself. He was so upset after being banished that he had started swimming without even thinking about where he was going. He certainly didn't want to end up in the Arktik where he heard the very water froze, forming jagged masses that could crush a shark!

Barkley flexed his flukes at Gray in irritation. "I'm hungry. How about we find some food?"

Finally, something they could agree on. It took a while, but they did find, and more importantly, *catch* some food. First Gray chased a small horde of cod toward

Barkley, who picked a few off. It was either a horde or upper drove. The dogfish thought it was an upper drove of eight or nine hundred. Gray didn't care as he was unable to catch even one since the small horde or upper drove was fast-moving and left the area quickly. But Barkley returned the favor by finding a lower cluster of sailfish. One muscular game fish didn't know what hit it as Gray pounced from below, taking most of it down with an enormous bite.

"Any cod left?" Gray asked after he'd finished off the last of the sailfish.

"You know, sailfish work out constantly. They think their bodies are temples. You might learn from that kind of thinking," Barkley told Gray while jabbing Gray's stomach with his tail.

"Hey, I'm big cartilaged!"

Barkley swam away, leading Gray in a slightly different direction. What was he doing?

"By the way, I'll pick the way we're heading, since it's my exile!" Gray told his friend, perhaps a little too vehemently, as he corrected their course.

"Right. What grade did you get in navigation class again?" Barkley asked innocently.

Oh, now he was playing dirty. Gray had taken the navigation test immediately after eating a puffer fish which had *not* gone down well. It felt as if the fish were inflating in his stomach, which cramped violently the entire day. The galling part was that he got *lost* during the exam! Miss Lamprey knew Gray was sick, which she took into account, but he got a poor grade that cycle.

The truth was Gray didn't know where he was going. For the first time in his life, he was swimming without a purpose. That scared him. Before, if he was unsure of what to do, he'd ask his mom. But he couldn't do that anymore. He was about to confess this to Barkley when the dogfish whispered a fearful "Uh-oh."

There were four sharks swimming in a tight pack; a thresher, a bull, a sawfish, and a great white. Miss Lamprey said great whites should be left alone in the open ocean. She said they hunted other sharkkind, even when they weren't hungry. For fun.

"Umm, Gray? How about we make like a sea frog and scoot?" suggested Barkley.

It was a good idea. But too late.

The four sharks fanned out and swam toward them.

CHAPTER 8

THE SHARKS WEREN'T ATTACKING. YET. THEY were in a strong defensive position, though.

"Oh, I don't like this one bit. We're jelly drifters here!" Barkley exclaimed. Gray and Barkley began swimming in a slow figure-eight pattern that would let them speed away in case trouble started. Gray was larger than any of the four by a few tail-tips, but the biggest fish wasn't always the winner in the Big Blue. That much even he knew.

The four sharkkind slowed their advance and hovered against the current. They were barely five tail strokes away. For a moment the only sound was the slow current swishing past their flanks.

"So," said the great white. "Any luck hunting?"

Barkley jumped in before Gray could reply, "Nope. Just seeing the sights. We're moving through. Sorry if this is your territory."

"Oh, it's not!" piped in the sawfish. He stopped talking when the white gave him a look. The great white was definitely the leader. Now that the group was so close, Gray could see they were pups like he and Barkley. If any were older than their twelve summers, it wasn't by much. An uncomfortable silence descended on them all. The thresher girl, who seemed nice, gave a worried look to the great white and indicated they should leave. He nodded and the four were about to turn.

For some reason Gray didn't want them to go. "So, what are your names? This is my friend Barkley and I'm Gray."

"I'm Snork!" replied the sawfish shark, a little too eagerly for anyone in either group. He was about to swim forward, maybe in greeting, but maybe for a sneak attack.

"Whoa, whoa, whoa! Snork, is it? Keep your distance, okay?" Barkley told the sawfish, whose nose looked sharp and deadly, chock-full of pointy spikes on either edge. Neither of them wanted to be filleted, so caution was a good thing.

The girl thresher didn't like this one bit. "You seem kind of rude, Barkley—is it?" she asked sarcastically, saying "is it" just like Barkley had, mocking him. This made Gray smile, which she saw and continued, "Snork's just being friendly, you know."

"Yeah," Gray piled on, "Snork's just being friendly."

Wow, if looks could send you to the Sparkle Blue,

Gray would have begun his eternal swim on the spot.

It turned out that Barkley's venomous stare was hilarious to the four sharks from the other group, and they laughed. "Oh, so now I'm the big flipper?" Barkley asked everyone. "I'm just being safe, you know!" For some reason this struck everyone as even funnier.

"You're hilarious!" exclaimed Snork, snorting as he laughed, making Barkley and Gray chortle along with everyone else. Pretty soon Gray's sides hurt he was laughing so much. It took a moment for everyone to catch their breath and introduce themselves properly.

Aside from Snork, the great white leader was Striiker, Shell was the big bull shark, and then there was Mari, who seemed pretty interested in Gray when he said he was a reef shark, but that could have been his imagination. Mari had that really cool thresher's tail, bent back at an angle that just looked awesome. Gray wondered if it made her faster.

"You're really a reef shark?" Mari asked.

"That's what my mom tells me," he joked. Of course he was a reef shark. What else would he be?

"They must grow them real big by that reef of yours," commented Shell. The bull was quieter than the rest. He seemed okay, though.

Barkley grew suspicious. "Enough about our reef. Where do you live?"

Now Striiker gave Barkley the stink eye. "Why do you want to know where we live?"

"Just making conversation." Barkley swished his tail in a way that told Gray he was agitated. "Any reason you're so nervous?"

"I'm not nervous. Any reason *you're* so nervous?" Striiker shot right back.

Mari swam between them, taking position by Gray's right. "Okay you two, enough," she said. "We're not part of any shiver, if that's what you're thinking. We're four friends who swim together because it's safer here if you do that."

"So, you're like a rogue quad?" Gray asked. Barkley waved his tail for him to stop.

Striiker was genuinely puzzled. "Rogue quad? Is that even a thing?"

"I love it!" Snork exclaimed.

Gray explained, "Barkley told this shark we were a rogue pair when he got flustered."

"Aww, did you have to go there?" Barkley said, flipping his fins in embarrassment. "I thought that giant tiger was going to kill us! A flipper named Thrash."

There was an immediate chill in the water. Their new acquaintances moved back a couple of tail strokes from Barkley and Gray. "You know Thrash? Are you friends with Thrash?" Striiker asked evenly.

Gray answered, "Like Barkley said, he attacked us. So, no, we're not friends." He proceeded to tell the entire story of their meeting with Thrash.

Barkley added a lot of description to the fight. Gray wasn't sure it was all true, but it sure sounded good. He ended with, " . . . and then that muck-sucker asked us to be a part of his gang, and I was like, 'no way, lagoon scum, we're a rogue pair and way too cool for your dumb shiver!' And we let him see our tails when we left." Barkley waved his tail in a derisive manner. It was kind of embarrassing. Almost no one believed that's what happened. Almost.

"You may be the coolest sharks, ever," Snork whispered in wonder.

Striiker shook his head. "And on that note . . . " He rolled a slow turn, beckoning Mari and the other three sharks away from Gray and Barkley. Mari didn't move, sizing them up, instead.

"They did fight Thrash, and they're still here," Mari told Striiker, who turned around. He didn't seem happy.

The bull shark agreed. "And they're not with Goblin."

Striiker glared at Snork before he could add anything, then frowned at both Mari and Shell. "We just met them today! How do we know they can be trusted?"

"How do we know *you* can be trusted?" Barkley huffed. "By the way, what are we talking about?"

Gray had a pretty good idea and nodded to Mari to continue.

"The reason they're still swimming the Big Blue is because there were two of them against Thrash. The reason we're still around is because we four look out for each other. I think six would be better than four," Mari explained.

Shell nodded in agreement. Barkley wasn't so sure. Striiker seemed annoyed but not totally against the idea. And Snork? Well, Snork was being friendly again. "Come on! With six sharks we could be a real shiver! A leader with Five in the Line!" he said.

The great white shook his head. "If we wanted that we could have all stayed in our shivers. Mostly." Striiker gave a guilty glance to Shell, who for some reason looked away. He continued, "The one reason we like each other is because we aren't in shivers, which we know from experience is bad!"

"Hey, not all shivers are bad," Barkley protested.

"Yeah, we came from a great shiver," Gray told the four.

"The six of us could be a good shiver! A great shiver, even!" Snork almost bounced in the water as he got more and more excited, flexing his flippers back and forth. "And I have the perfect name! Rogue Shiver!"

And so, on the swim to their new homewaters, Rogue Shiver was born.

CHAPTER 9

THE PALE MOON'S GLOW LIT THE WATERS WITH a soft and eerie light. Gray sped toward the drove of snapper, slowing just enough to let them see him streaking their way. The group of fish angled away from his open maw—right between the walls of a cramped canyon where Rogue Shiver was waiting! The plan worked to perfection once again, and Gray was able to munch his share of snapper as they fled in the return direction after the rest caught theirs.

"We are getting so good at this!" Barkley remarked, finishing off a plump and juicy fish.

Gray nodded. Who would have thought that what had started out with the worst day of his life would turn into the best time of his life? It had been two weeks since Gray and Barkley formed Rogue Shiver with their new friends. After some initial wariness, mostly from Striiker, the group now mixed easily. They learned many things about each other, except for the whale in the water. The one topic nobody brought up was why each was swimming the Big Blue and not in another shiver.

"I'm stuffed," said Snork. "We never ate this well when there were just four of us!" It turned out Snork was nearly thirteen and a half, the oldest of the group by six months, although he didn't act like it. Striiker and Mari were twelve like Gray and Barkley, and Shell had turned thirteen just last month.

"It's probably a good time for hunting or something," Gray said.

Striiker harrumphed. "Let's go home. We don't want to be seen by Goblin Shiver's patrols." For some reason, if anything was more annoying to the great white than having his leadership questioned, it was Gray being nice to him.

"Their name was much cooler when it was Riptide Shiver," remarked Snork as he followed. "Since Goblin changed it, now *we* have the best shiver name in the whole Big Blue."

They actually had performed a shiver creation ceremony. Snork insisted. Even Striiker went along with it, probably because he got to be leader. The others voted themselves in the order they had been subconsciously swimming in. Mari was elected first, Shell second, and Snork third. Gray was chosen as fourth in the Line. Mari wanted to vote Gray higher, much higher in fact, but he wouldn't hear of it. It did seem pretty funny that Snork—

now that he knew Snork—was technically supposed to be tougher than him. Gray let it slide. He hadn't been in the open ocean for even one moon, and he knew the others were better suited toward making decisions.

Besides, Gray was happy to wait until the Tuna Run when he would rejoin his mother and Coral Shiver. Gray wanted to ask his new friends to come to the reef but hadn't found the right time. He didn't tell this to anyone, though, because he hadn't mentioned it to Barkley yet. The dogfish's mood was *not* good when he was chosen as Rogue Shiver's fifth.

"Are you kidding me?" his friend wailed. "There are only six of us, total! That's just embarrassing!" But when Mari asked whether he would rather be fifth in the Line or the only general member of Rogue Shiver, Barkley grumbled "Fine. Fifth. Great," and swam away. It took an entire day to calm the dogfish down.

Their new home was only a short swim away and well hidden. Towering brown and blue-greenie waved majestically, forming a wall that made everyone feel safe. You could enter unseen by swimming berneath a short tunnel formed by a fallen cliff. And there was the perfect hiding spot. It was an old landshark ship, *really* old from what Barkley told them. And big!

The ship had three levels, and when it had ridden the chop-chop, humans used wooden planks called "oars" to move the bulky thing through the water! Aside from a large crack in the bottom of the ship now, it was through these oar openings that a nice current flowed, allowing easy breathing. This was much better than sleeping in open water where you could be spotted, or down in the greenie where you could get something in your gills. There was plenty of space inside, although one room on the end was filled with shiny yellow disks that spilled everywhere because the wooden boxes they were packed into had rotted through. No one liked that area, as the moldy boxes left a tang in the water you could taste, unlike the rest of the ship.

Even though the ship lay three times the depth of the reef, there was still good light from the sun and moon. But it wasn't like the reef where other dwellers would talk with the shiver. Here the shellheads, lumos, fish, and urchins stayed out of the way when Rogue Shiver was around. Gray tried to ask a sea dragon if she knew Yappy, but the little dweller slalomed into the greenie without saying a word. He hadn't thought he'd miss speaking with other dwellers, but he did.

Only when Gray and his new shiver were by the wreck did they relax completely. It had been a good day. No, a great day. Gray found himself staring at Mari's sleek thresher tail as they went inside the landshark ship.

Unfortunately, Barkley saw this and whispered, "Mari cuts a nice wake, eh?"

He felt his face color. "She's okay, I guess."

They hung around the main cabin, enjoying the cool current streaming through the ship. Gray decided on the spot. It was finally time to tell the rest of Rogue Shiver how he got here.

"You've all heard of the Tuna Run?" he asked.

Striiker snorted. "I've been there twice!" Others in the group rolled their eyes. Apparently the great white spoke about this a little too often.

"Well, I think I should tell you how I got here and why I'm mentioning it now," Gray told everyone.

"Everyone's tired, Gray." Barkley swished his tail furiously. "We don't need to hear any of your long, boring stories." But Gray was determined and told the entire tale. After he was finished, Mari, Striiker, Shell, and Snork stared at Barkley with a newfound respect.

The dogfish misread the situation. "What? Is there snapper between my teeth?" he asked, genuinely clueless.

Snork tapped his saw bill on Barkley's head. "You are the best friend a fin could have!"

Even the normally quiet Shell remarked, "Not many sharkkind would leave their home like that."

Gray never thought he'd see the day when Barkley was speechless, but that day had come. The dogfish stuttered, actually embarrassed by the attention. "Yeah well, that's the way I roll. Anyway, we're talking about Gray who still hasn't said what any of this has to do with Tuna Run! So?" Barkley gave Gray a friendly bump in the flank with his snout.

"My mom wants me to find her at the Tuna Run. If I can prove I'm a good hunter, they'll let me back in."

The reaction wasn't what Gray expected.

"You're leaving?" asked Mari.

"I knew they were just acting like our friends!" huffed Striiker. "They only needed a place to stay for a while."

Shell stared at both of them as Snork said in a trembling voice, "Is that true, Gray?"

Gray had enough of Striiker. "You know, you're a real tail bender! I've been nothing but nice, and you just think the worst of me!"

"Tell me I'm wrong!" roared Striiker

Gray was ready to rumble, butting Striiker against the hull of the landshark ship. "If you'd let me finish, I was going to say you could all come back to the reef and be a part of Coral Shiver, you great, big krillhead!"

Striiker was speechless for a moment. "You'd do that for us?" he asked in wonder. "For me, even?"

Gray was taken aback by the vulnerability of the great white. "If you promised not to be such a flipper, then yes."

"But if you think you'd be leading, or even in the Line, you'd be wrong," said Barkley a little too loudly. He had taken up position above Gray and was still amped up and ready to fight the great white. "I mean, maybe one day, maybe. But you know how it is with new members. Take it from your fifth." This got a chuckle from Striiker, which released all the tension among them. Pretty soon everyone was chattering excitedly, with Barkley telling the other four all the great things about Coral Shiver's reef.

But everything took an odd turn when Shell asked, "So it was still there when you guys went back?"

"Went back when?" asked Gray.

"The day when Barkley was named fifth and swam off," the bull shark answered. "We thought you went for a visit or something. Some of us do that, from time to time. We didn't know you had been barrished."

"No, our home is farther than that," Gray told him.

"And the reef's been there since Tyro swam past it," Barkley guffawed. "Why wouldn't it still be there?"

Everyone grew quiet. A bad feeling prickled up Gray's spine. He looked at Mari for an explanation, but she shook her head and didn't say anything.

Striiker swam forward a bit. "You mentioned you were in a shiver by a reef when you fought Thrash. You shouldn't have done that."

Barkley shook his head. "Gray didn't say *where* our homewaters were."

"They found mine," Snork whispered in a haunted voice. The happy-go-lucky sawfish was trembling. "They find every shiver they hear about."

"Mostly, we're from shivers that Goblin found," said Shell sadly. "He's at war with my old shiver, Razor Shiver. The only reason we're still alive is because we have more mariners than Goblin. Not because he doesn't want to destroy those homewaters."

Mari was upset and didn't seem to want to speak, but Gray motioned her to tell him what she was thinking.

"Thrash is dumb, but if he told Goblin you were from a reef where he could find new recruits, he *will* find your reef."

"Then what?" Gray asked, growing frantic. "What would he do?"

Snork's voice was faraway and reedy when he broke the silence. He whispered, "They eat anyone who doesn't join."

CHAPTER 10

GRAY AND BARKLEY LEFT IMMEDIATELY FOR THE reef and didn't speak, conserving their energy on the long trip. After two nonstop days swimming with no food or rest, they finally reached the Coral Shiver home-waters. Gray saw that the greenie path into the reef was intact.

But it was quiet. Very quiet.

There was usually noise by the reef. Keen shark senses picked up the sounds and disturbances caused by dwellers and other sharkkind talking or swimming. When you weren't hunting, you'd ignore these as back-ground noise. Now all Gray felt, all he heard, was the gentle tide swishing the greenie back and forth. There were no snatches of conversation, or shouting, or tail strokes from any ocean dweller. It set him on edge. Gray's heart was pounding so hard, it felt as if it would hammer its way out of his body.

"Follow me," he whispered.

The entire reef was still and silent. When he got closer, he noticed there were a few tiny, darting fish about, but not many. The larger dwellers had been scared away. Or eaten. He could smell the faint scent of blood everywhere. The beautiful corals and greenie were gouged and torn, as if hit by a mighty undersea storm. A few urchins and anemones were there, but faded their colors into muted browns and grays, the better to hide themselves. For a moment neither Gray nor Barkley said anything, hushed by the devastation around them. Gray had expected the worst, but it still didn't prepare him for this. The reef was totally destroyed.

"Do you think everyone..." Barkley left the question hanging in the water.

"Mom! Mom!" yelled Gray, startling the dogfish. No one answered, though.

"All of them?" Barkley asked himself in a dazed voice. "How can...how?

"NO!" Gray sped around the entire reef but it was the same everywhere. Desolation and stillness. Gray and Barkley cried by the edge of the reef, where they had gone after the drove of bluefin. It was quite some time before either could speak.

"This is my fault," Gray told Barkley.

"Gray—"

He cut his friend off. "If I had listened to you none of this would have happened! If I had listened to Mom! If I—"

Barkley gave him a sudden stinging tail slap to the flank. "You didn't do this! You. Did. Not."

This didn't make Gray feel any better. He knew deep inside that this was his burden to carry. I'm sorry, Mom, he thought silently as the slow tide carried his tears away.

"Gray? Barkley?" asked a small voice. They looked to where a few sad strands of greenie were still in place. There! Something moved. Gray and Barkley tensed, scared and alert.

Out poked Yappy's head. "Is it really you?"

Barkley exhaled loudly. "Yappy! You nearly scared us to death!"

Gray quickly swam up to Yappy and asked loudly, "Who did this? Have you seen my mother? Where is everyone?"

The little sea dragon zipped back into the greenie. "Stop yelling at me!" he squeaked.

Barkley nipped at Gray's tail, almost getting bitten as a result. The dogfish couldn't believe it and yelled, "What's wrong with you? Yappy's our friend." Gray saw the look in Barkley's eyes and was ashamed.

Yappy poked his head out of the greenie again. "Really, Barkley? I always thought you didn't like me!"

"No, Yappy. Sometimes I get annoyed and take stuff out on you. Sorry," said the dogfish. "Do you know where our families are and what happened?"

"I don't know where your cousins are, Barkley. They were on the other side of the reef, so I didn't see. The shiver, they tried to fight. They tried. But there were so many. So many."

"My mom?" asked Gray fearfully.

"I'm not sure." The little sea dragon choked back a sob. "I ran and hid! I'm a coward!"

"You're not a coward!" Barkley told him. "The shiver—were they taken?"

"No! They got away!" Yappy told them. Gray's heart leapt as Yappy continued. "Atlas was shouting, 'Go! Go! We'll meet at the Tuna Run!'" The sea dragon brightened a little. "You shoulda seen Atlas! He wanted everyone to leave, but Overbiter stayed with him, flank to flank! They held them off as Quickeyes and Onyx led everyone away! Sent at least three of them to the Sparkle Blue! But then..." Sadness returned to Yappy's eyes.

Gray couldn't speak, so Barkley prodded in a low voice, "Then?"

"They both were eaten."

Gray felt a hotness growing inside him. A reddish haze descended over his eyes as he thought of someone eating sharks from his shiver family. "Who did that?" Gray asked in a deathly quiet voice.

The little sea dragon's eyes grew misty. "They came at high moon when everybody was resting. But not me. I saw them. I saw ..."

"Yappy! Saw who?" Gray asked his voice rising, Barkley gave him a look when the sea dragon cringed.

"Saw who?" the dogfish asked in a soothing tone.

The sea dragon answered in a shaky whisper, "Bull sharks. They were bulls."

Barkley was struck dumb with a look of disbelief. Gray swam over, but not too fast or close this time. He kept his voice low so he wouldn't scare the sea dragon off. "Yappy, this is no time for stories. Who really did this?"

"STORIES?" he yelled into Gray's face. "Look around, you big lumpfish! Two of my sisters were eaten!" Gray actually backed away from the tiny sea dragon's rage and grief. Yappy got hold of himself. "I'm sorry I yelled. But they were definitely bull sharks. The one who ate Paxson had a weird scar on his snout. Looked like a clam shell."

Paxson was the sea dragon's oldest sister. She had always made fun of her brother for talking with Gray and Barkley. Now she was gone.

"Do you want to come with us?" Barkley asked. "We have another place."

The sea dragon shook his head. "My family's leaving. We have cousins in the Dark Blue. We'll stay with them for a while." Yappy's eyes grew hard for a moment. "When we find those bulls, we'll get them. You'll see." The diminutive sea dragon flicked his flippers in a wave good-bye and left. "See you around. Maybe."

Barkley shook his head. "Yappy and his giant cousins getting revenge on a shiver of bulls. If it wasn't today that would be funny."

"But it is today," said Gray. "And it's a good idea. We'll find who did this and somehow, someway—"

Barkley flicked a fin at Gray. "Whoa, whoa," he said. "Didn't you hear the good news? Yappy didn't see our families get taken or eaten. He said the shiver escaped! We'll go to the Tuna Run and find them." Gray was about to ask if Barkley really believed that everyone was still alive and there would be a big, happy reunion at the Tuna Run. His friend saw the question in his eyes and answered before Gray could say anything. "I have to believe that," he said. "We both do."

Barkley was right. No matter what, their families would be at the Tuna Run.

They would find them. Or swim the Sparkle Blue trying.

GOBLIN SHIVER

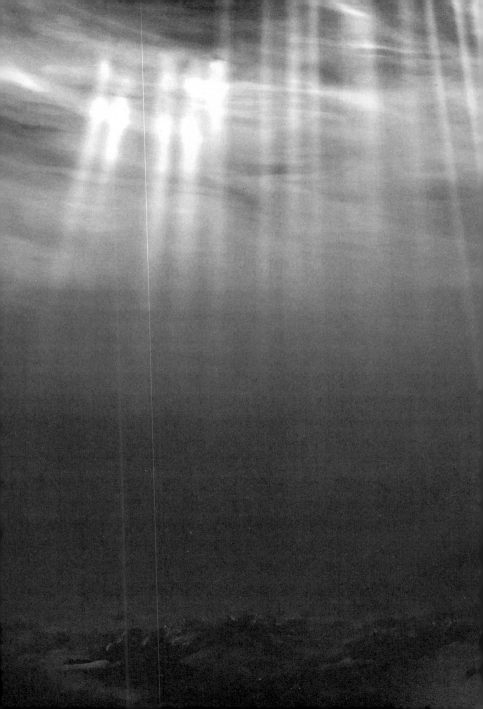

CHAPTER 11

THE SWIM BACK WAS QUIET. GRAY WAS WORRIED sick about his mother. But there was another thought that cut through this sadness, and he was ashamed that it terrified him more than anything else. Gray was homeless now. Barkley was also, of course. And the dogfish was certainly worried about his family. But Gray's overriding feeling wasn't sadness, anger, or confusion. It was fear that he had no place to go. And this made him feel awful because he was only thinking about himself. Again.

Before this, after his banishment was over, Gray's exile would have turned into an adventure he'd tell stories about around the reef. But now his mother was missing, and there was no Coral Shiver reef to go back to and he was petrified.

Gray could feel that Barkley was also scared, but grief was the biggest sensation coming from him right now. He grew mortified when he realized the his friend could probably feel his state of mind, too. "I'm the worst shark ever," Gray muttered.

They reached the edge of the Rogue Shiver homewaters, where they were met by Mari. Her silhouette was easy to spot with the sun shining overhead. She raced over. "Are you okay?" Then she saw the looks on their faces and knew everything wasn't okay. "I'm so sorry. I hate Goblin!"

"It wasn't him," Barkley told her. "They were bulls."

"Oh, no! Please don't tell Shell that!"

Gray was going to ask why, when the big bull steamed toward them. "Striiker saw Thrash on patrol! We should get back to the wreck and hover low."

They began swimming, picking up their pace with steady, powerful tail strokes. They were nearly home when they saw Striiker and Snork. They were being circled by at least ten other sharks!

"Goblin Shiver!" Mari exclaimed.

There was no trouble picking Goblin out of the pack. He was as large as Gray, but all muscle, his teeth flashing in a harsh grin. Striiker and Snork had nowhere to run. The seabed was clearly in sight, and the greenie and rock formations in the area were too sparse to hide in.

"We can make it home without being seen if we stay away," whispered Shell.

"Shell's making some very good sense," said Barkley, tapping Gray's side with his tail.

Mari bristled. "We can't just leave them!"

Then they heard sharks laughing and Goblin's booming voice carrying through the current. "If you don't join us, we'll rip your pointy-nosed friend to pieces in front of you!"

That did it. "You guys can go. I'm not." Gray swam toward Goblin, who taunted the sawfish by nipping at his tail as his other shiver sharks laughed.

Gray picked up his pace by ferociously whipping his tail back and forth. He lost speed blasting two whitetips out of his way. Gray hit the great white in the side, doing no real damage but forcing him from Snork. There was yelling and screaming and total confusion for a few seconds. Gray saw that Barkley, Mari, and Shell had followed him into the melee! His heart pounded with pride and fear as the two shivers faced one another, ready to fight. Rogue was outnumbered about three to one, but at least they weren't surrounded anymore.

"Who the heck are you?" shouted Goblin.

"Come find out!" Gray yelled back.

It seemed like the shiver leader would surely attack, but a mako got his attention and whispered something only he could hear. The mako was black as night with eyes even blacker. She stared at Gray as if she was looking inside him. Inwardly Gray shivered and wondered why he was doing so. Goblin calmed down, curiously looking him over from snout to tail tip.

"Told ya he was different," said Thrash, off to

one side. Goblin silenced him with a hard look. Gray watched Goblin, who was distracted by the mako speaking low and urgently to him. Gray probably would have been distracted, too. Even in this life-threatening situation, he couldn't help but notice that the mako was stunningly beautiful. Every now and again her sleek, black upper half would reflect the sunlight from above, making her skin shimmer with color like a rainbow.

"All right, all right," Goblin told the mako, irritated. He swirled his fins and made an incredibly quick turn to face Gray. This great white was much faster than Striiker! Gray was lucky he'd caught the big fish by surprise, or he might have ended up swimming the Sparkle Blue. "So, how's your day been? Good?"

The change in tone caught everyone by surprise. Gray didn't have the first clue what to say. Striiker shoved in front of him. "Like I told you, we were just leaving, Goblin."

"I wasn't talking to you, flipper," the larger great white told him. He flicked his tail dismissively at Striiker, who gritted his teeth at the insult. Goblin looked right at Gray. "You! Who are you and what are you doing here?"

"Don't be a turtle. Say something," Barkley whispered to Gray, who slapped him quiet with his tail. He didn't need the dogfish's special brand of humor right now.

"I was—" as Gray spoke he was reminded that he had

just come from his destroyed home and missing mother. He was nearly overcome with emotion. I'm going to bawl like a pup in front of everyone, Gray thought. Way to make a tough impression.

Mari, sensing his hesitation, took over the conversation. "He's lost his home and family, Goblin. He and the dogfish were passing through when we found them."

The mako swam smoothly in front of Goblin and gently scraped against Gray's side. It felt wonderful. "You poor fin," she said. "You must feel so alone. I'm Velenka, by the way."

Mari stared daggers at the mako and gave her a quick slap with the elongated upper lobe of her tail. "He's not alone, Velenka. He's with us!" She stared defiantly. That was odd. Mari seemed to know both Velenka and Goblin.

Snork chose this time to exclaim, "You attacked his family just like you attacked mine!"

Goblin struggled to keep his temper. "I asked you to join us and your leader said no. That was his choice, not mine."

"You're a murderer!" cried Snork.

"A realist," Goblin insisted. "I won't let my shiver starve, and I won't share what little food there is in these waters. Your leadership failed you." The great white was very much in control as he stared down the sawfish.

"Rogue Shiver forever!" Snork yelled.

Goblin chuckled, joined by everyone else on his side. "Rogue Shiver?" The great white shook his head at Finn.

"I should have known you were involved when the reports came in of sharks hunting in our territory without permission, Mari."

Barkley and Gray looked at each other. Goblin *did* know Mari!

That wasn't the end of the surprises, not by a long shot. It turned out both Striiker and Mari were former members of Riptide Shiver and had left after Goblin became the leader. In fact, they'd left right when he renamed the shiver after himself. Mari's mother and father were members too, before they died. She blamed Goblin for the loss of many shark lives, including her father's.

The big great white was offended. "That wasn't my fault," he said in a quiet voice. "Your father was on a patrol, and Razor Shiver attacked us. I'm sorry about him, just like I'm sorry when we lose anyone from the shiver!"

Goblin seemed genuinely upset, which confused Gray. He expected the great white to be evil and nothing more. Certainly not a fin with feelings. Velenka saw his reaction. "I see you've heard Mari's lies about our shiver," she remarked. The mako moved closer, as if to stroke Gray's flank, but stopped when Mari glared. "Goblin Shiver is about family. We protect our friends and our hunting grounds. Is there anything wrong with that?" Valenka asked Gray, her big black eyes boring into him. He couldn't find anything wrong with it.

Gray turned to Mari. "So Razor Shiver sent your father to Sparkle Blue?"

"Goblin and Razor have been fighting for years. They won't stop until everyone's dead!"

"But the bulls did that. Just like they did to Coral Shiver," said Gray.

Goblin shook his head at Gray. "Mari needed someone to blame, so I let her blame me. Should we leave our territory and wander the Big Blue homeless? No. We stand and fight."

Velenka looked pointedly at Gray. "Don't you want revenge on the ones who destroyed your home?"

"I do."

Barkley grew alarmed. "Gray, no! We'll meet our families at the Tuna Run!"

"If they're alive," he answered. "But we need to survive until then."

Goblin smiled a toothy smile. "Then come with us. But I won't let you hunt in our territory. You join the shiver or leave the area."

"Oh, really?" Striiker asked sarcastically. "You'll just forgive and forget? You must be pretty desperate."

Goblin's eyes flared with anger, but his answer came calmly as he looked at Mari and Striiker. "We need to band together and put aside our differences, so I forgive you both." Next he flicked his tail at Snork. "I'm sorry I threatened you. It was Striiker who made me angry. You can leave here in peace or come along. Your choice."

Barkley looked absolutely pained. "Gray, this is crazy."

"It gives us the best chance to get to the Tuna Run and find everyone," he told his friend. "And I want to fight the bulls. Sorry, Barkley."

Shell, who was a bull himself, had been silent for the entire exchange. Now he asked, "What about me? Can I join?"

Mari looked horrified.

Goblin swam around the bull, taking his measure. "I recognize you. You've battled against us." Shell gave a terse nod. "You'd fight your own shiver? Why?"

There was a long silence. "You don't need to know why. You just need to know I'd fight against Razor and anyone who swims at his flank."

The great white nodded. "That's good enough for me."

CHAPTER 12

THE FORMER MEMBERS OF ROGUE SHIVER SWAM into their new homewaters at moonrise. It wasn't like the Coral Shiver reef or the landshark ship, which relied on greenie to hide their location. This wasn't hidden at all. Since ancient times this shiver had been an unquestioned power in the North Atlantis, and their location was well-known in the Big Blue. Gray wondered aloud why the shiver didn't just move if they were being attacked.

"So we can move from one place to the next like jelly drifters?" Goblin asked, shaking his massive head from side to side. "My shiver has claimed this territory from the time of Tyro. We're going nowhere."

"That's truer than you know," muttered Mari. Both Striiker and Barkley stifled their snorts.

Goblin didn't hear, or he pretended not to hear, and continued, "Besides, don't you think this place is worth fighting for?" The great white said the last as they swam over the crest of a hill, which revealed a massive, sloping cliff face that glittered with different colored greenie, each on a separate terrace. The greenie was grown and tended this way! Incredible! The entire Coral Shiver reef could have easily fit inside a small portion of this place. At the floor of the cliff, long greenie grew in thick strands that were forever scrubbing the lower crags, flowing back and forth with the currents. The expanse in front of the cliffs where the shiver-gathering area was located was even larger, with huge pylons of rock and coral. There were whales here! And schools of giant manta rays! Both Gray and Barkley's mouths hung open in wonder.

"I think I just swallowed a tooth," Barkley whispered.

Gray nodded to his friend. "You and me both."

"Wow," said Snork, waggling his serrated nose as he looked this way and that. Barkley dodged the dangerous snout and decided to move a body length away. The sawfish had ended up coming with them. Gray was glad for that. Snork was a genuinely good fish. Striiker and Mari, having seen the shiver homewaters before, didn't react much.

Goblin proudly swished his tail as if he'd personally carved out the cliffs and planted the terraced greenie himself. "This is my home. Our home."

Velenka swam over. "Now, I don't know about where you lived before, but there are a few rules we follow."

"Hmph!" Goblin grumbled. "We do it to make the dwellers feel like they have a say, but sharkkind run things around here."

"Of course we do," the mako said before turning to Gray and Barkley. "In this area we don't hunt. It's a safe zone for everyone."

"Sure," Barkley agreed. "That's how it was where we lived."

Goblin jumped back into the conversation. "Ah, but if a dweller leaves this area you can take it as a meal if you're hungry." The great white ground his triangular teeth together and smiled.

"Really?" Gray asked. This sounded a bit awful. How could you talk to someone one minute and eat him or her the next?

Mari knew what he was thinking and said to everyone, "Yup! You can be having a perfectly nice conversation with a dweller, and if it drifts outside the magical marker, you can have it for lunch! Literally. Isn't Goblin Shiver nice?"

"We aren't supposed to be nice!" Goblin answered sharply. "Nice fish get eaten! We're only as strong as our mariners, and they need to be fed."

While Gray liked Mari, he thought Goblin made a good point. If Coral Shiver had been stronger, maybe it would still exist. He pushed the thought from his head.

The rest of the day was spent on a tour with Goblin and Velenka. There certainly was a lot to see. Thrash went out on patrol with four other shiver sharks. They met other members of Goblin's Line returning from another patrol: Streak, Churn, and Ripper. Ripper was a giant hammerhead and Goblin's first. He had so many scars it was hard to find a section of his massive body that was unmarred. Streak, a shiny blue shark that seemed really angry, was third in the Line. Mari told him that Streak acted that way all the time. But she said it very quietly, so the blue wouldn't hear. Fourth was Churn, a whitetip who said, "Learn to love patrolling, pups," and laughed as he passed.

"You've been scratched," Goblin told Gray. "Looks like my hide has some bite of its own, eh?" Gray looked at his flank down by the tail. It was gashed slightly, blood seeping from the wound. At the reef he would have let it heal on its own.

But Goblin said, "Go with Velenka and get that fixed."

Mari immediately said, "I'll swim him over there."

But the great white shook his head. "No, you won't."

The thresher glared but bobbed her head to the shiver leader and obeyed. Velenka flicked her tail for Gray to follow. With a last look at Barkley, he went.

"You have no clue what getting a scratch *fixed* means, do you?" she asked with a chuckle. Gray didn't but wasn't about to let the mako know that. He swam past a small reef almost entirely covered by starfish. There must have been thousands in a pile, and these stars were much bigger than the ones at the reef. Everything was bigger! It took real effort for Gray not to gawk like a pup at all they passed. She continued, "By treaty, any dweller who dies in the area is given to the bottom feeders, including shark-kind. Waste not, want not." The rule was the same in his homewaters, but it always made Gray a little queasy. He knew the muck-suckers were just doing their job cleaning the Big Blue. And he guessed it was better than seeing the carcass of one of your shivermates slowly decay into nothingness. But it was still creepy. "In return, they do things for us."

They swam over to an area where there were many fish, urchins, and crabs. There also seemed to be a few recently injured fish, but amazingly, their wounds had been *repaired* somehow. Gray had never seen anything like it before.

"The shiver requests help!" she announced loudly before turning to him. "I have to go find payment. Be back soon."

A large yellow surgeonfish came over and swam around Gray's cut. "Ah, not too bad," she said. "We'll have you in and out in no time. I need a doctor here!" A doctor fish joined them and began nibbling on the edge of his wound.

"Hey! What's the big idea?" Gray shouted.

The surgeonfish swam in front of his left eye. "My name is Oceana, and I'm your surgeonfish. Hold still. We can't fix this if you move around."

Oceana flicked out razor-sharp spines from the

back of her tail and gently cut the ragged edge of Gray's wound. Another doctor fish joined the first and ate the remains. Gray tried not to move as this tickled a little. It was also kind of disgusting.

"We have surgeon and doctor fish at the reef. *Had*, I mean," Gray said. "But I've never seen any do this!"

Oceana chuckled. "Not every surgeon or doctor fish can. You have to be trained, usually in an ancient shiver's homewaters. The best are the shivers that allied with humans in the olden days."

"You mean landsharks?" Gray asked. "Sharks and landsharks were friends?"

The surgeonfish nodded at his amazement. "*Landshark*. Such a rustic term. Anyway, we have the finest treatment for wounded sharkkind and dwellers in all the Atlantis. This is literally cutting edge, and you wouldn't see it if you grew up in some out of the way backwater. What we're doing is clearing away the dead and infected skin so we can suture the cut. Hold still." Gray didn't want to ask any more questions, as he already felt like a jelly-brain, but *suture* the cut? What did that word even mean?

He watched and found out. When the gash was cleaned, it did seem to feel better. An old sea turtle swam up carrying a crab on its back. The turtle hovered as the shellhead, with amazing dexterity, inserted and tied off several urchin spines, knitting both sides of the cut together. It was amazing!

In a moment Velenka came back with a fat haddock in her mouth. She chewed it several times and let it sink to the rock bottom as the crab finished its work. The doctor fish nibbled on the edges of the knitted wound, smoothing them. After they finished, the dwellers descended on the fresh fish.

"Paid in full," Velenka told Oceana and her assistants. The mako tapped the urchin spines in Gray's flank. "Those will work their way out, or you can come back and have them removed. But then you owe them a fish."

"Thanks," he said. The wound felt better, and the oozing blood had completely stopped.

"Come on," Velenka said to Gray. "Let me show you some of the shorter patrol routes. If you feel well enough, that is."

"Do I!" he told the mako. Gray wanted to see everything! Luckily, it seemed Mari and Striiker were completely wrong about Goblin Shiver.

CHAPTER 13

THE MOON HAD GONE THROUGH AN ENTIRE cycle since Rogue Shiver had joined Goblin Shiver. Most days were spent patrolling their territory and hunting. All the sharks from the shiver took turns swimming patrol routes, but there was always a large group protecting the homewaters. Other than a few probing patrols of their own, there was little sign of Razor Shiver. Gray hadn't seen a single bull.

"You think maybe the war is over?" he asked Barkley. "It has been very quiet." This was Gray's first time patrolling with the dogfish. He had been looking forward to it all week. His friends hadn't adapted to their new lives as well as Gray had to his. Mari and Striiker both seemed edgy or irritated most of the time. Other than a few meetings by the Speakers Rock for announcements or speeches by Goblin, Gray really didn't see his ex-shivermates at all. It seemed as though they were being intentionally kept apart.

"No, it's not over," answered Barkley, "and this isn't a war. It's more like a turf battle, which is why we didn't know anything about it. If there was a war—a real war—we would have heard something, even by the reef." The dogfish snapped up a mackerel that passed close to his mouth. "I think we should leave. I hear the Sific Ocean is nice. Goblin would never follow us all the way there," he told Gray while he munched on the fish.

"And what about your cousins?" Gray asked. "And my mom?"

"Easy. We sneak back through the territory when the time for the Tuna Run comes."

Gray could see Streak and Ripper in the distance, waiting to continue their patrol. "Let's talk about this some other time," he told the dogfish.

"Sure, Gray. Whatever." Barkley swam away without another word.

"Any trouble?" Streak asked.

"All quiet," Gray replied. The blue nodded, and the pair swam out.

"Well, well, well!" said Goblin, appearing from nowhere. "How's everything going?"

"Fine, Goblin." Gray grew wary. The shiver leader hadn't ever stopped to chat before.

"Follow me," the great white told him. They went to the edge of the central area and then a little farther. Suddenly Goblin turned and attacked! It was all Gray could do to evade his initial rush. Then they both spun a tight turn and rammed each other. Gray was dazed, then Goblin started laughing. "You don't know your own strength. For a young pup, you hit like Ripper!"

Gray was confused but couldn't help but puff with pride at the compliment. Ripper was a warrior, a true mariner. That much he knew from his short time here. "Umm, thanks."

"You've been with us a month now," Goblin said. "Are you getting your sea legs?"

"'Sea *legs*'?"

The great white chuckled. "Right, you're from the boonie-greenie." Gray was about to ask where the boonie-greenie was but thought better of it. "'Sea legs' is a landshark saying for getting used to the ocean. Humans sometimes get sick on their boats when the chop-chop is rough. When they get used to the waves, they say their landshark legs have turned into 'sea legs.' Get it?"

Gray understood very little of what Goblin was saying. Barkley would have definitely known. Maybe he should have paid a little more attention in Miss Lamprey's classes. In any case, an answer wasn't required.

"Did you know sharkkind used to talk with the humans? They even use some of our words!"

"Aww, come on," Gray said before he could stop himself.

But Goblin didn't get angry. "No, really. These home-waters have been led by great whites for thousands of years." Goblin thumped him on the head with his tail in a joking way. Gray didn't mind, though, as the shiver leader was talking and listening to him. That was something that Atlas never did. "In those days the entire Atlantis Ocean was part of an empire that ruled with an iron fin over all the seven seas."

Gray was fascinated. He listened as Goblin told him that an evil and corrupt mako empress by the name of Silander ruled everything from her giant kingdom in the Sific Ocean, which was a hundred times larger than Goblin Shivers homewaters. She ordered her brutal, armored *squaline*, which meant "fish soldier" in an ancient landshark language called Latin, to collect food from the shivers until everyone was starving. "*Squaline* is also where the concept of the Line comes from," Goblin noted. "But good shark-kind in the Indi, Arktik, and Atlantis oceans rose up against her empire. Riptide was formed back then, and it teamed with tattooed Indi Shiver to strike the first blow in a long war."

Gray was hesitant to interrupt but asked, "Tattooed Indi Shiver?"

"No, they're called Indi Shiver, *and* they have tattoos." Goblin saw that Gray didn't understand and explained further. "They mark themselves with designs on their bodies by having urchins crawl along their skin and release acid."

How cool was that? It was the most interesting story ever! Gray listened, totally captivated as Goblin described the pitched battle between *armadas* of sharkkind and dwellers on each side in the South Atlantis that broke Silander's power. It was fittingly called the Battle of Silander's End. After she lost, her own Line sent her to the Sparkle Blue. Then those sharkkind fought among themselves over who would lead, and the empire crumbled, never to rise again.

Gray just gaped. He couldn't believe he had never heard of this before. What kind of school was Miss Lamprey leading? They spent a month studying plankton! But Gray knew it wasn't her fault. The Caribbi sea was off the beaten path, and she probably didn't know anything about the Battle of Silander's End. Or maybe he wasn't paying attention that day in class. It was definitely one or the other.

"So, are there still big battle shivers with armadas of sharkkind?" Gray asked.

"No, they all splintered into smaller ones like here in the Atlantis. Some say Indi Shiver has a new pup king who wants to be emperor of the Big Blue. They say he's already taken over the Arktik."

Gray gasped. "Is it true?"

The great white chuckled. "No. These stories bubble

up every now and again. Ten years ago, a South Sific shiver was supposedly conquering everything. Somewhere far away, there's probably a story about me wanting to be emperor."

"Do you?"

The great white waggled a fin, pointing. "Can you guess how this part of the Big Blue got its name?" Goblin asked. Gray didn't know, and the story the great white told seemed even more unbelievable and made him forget his question. The Atlantis Ocean wasn't named after sharkkind after all. It was named for landsharks who called themselves Atlanteans! They lived on a faraway island. All the shivers, even when they fought each other, would protect Atlanteans if their ships sank in storms. In return, these landsharks taught them things, just like Oceana told him.

The Atlanteans were the ones who showed sharkkind how to repair battle wounds and even cure fever from the poisonous stings of urchins and jellies with algae and mosses from the ocean. They forged metal armor for sharkkind, with razor edges to cover fins, a spike for the tail, and protective plating for the flanks. Sometimes humans even swam into battle with sharks, protecting their dorsal topside while breathing air from a bladder made of animal skin! The humans who lived on Europa got jealous of the Atlanteans as they became more and more powerful and finally sank their island. They killed many sharks while doing that. Because of this treachery, all sharkkind vowed never to treat with humans ever again. Now any landsharks that came into the Big Blue were fair game.

"Although they're not really worth it, even the fatter ones," said Goblin as he made a face. "They're bony and don't taste good at all."

Goblin also told Gray about the measurements landsharks used. These measurements did seem useful, especially when comparing them against the mako standard of flippers and body lengths. It would be easier to tell someone that a drove of halibut was a thousand feet down than to describe it in tip-to-tails. Gray wondered how the landsharks could be so smart and so stupid at the same time. After generations and generations of sailing on the Big Blue, they still can't swim better than a turtle!

"Why are you telling me all this?" Gray asked.

Goblin smiled. "I see potential in you. Who knows, maybe one day you could be in the Line. Maybe even my first." The initial emotion that hit Gray wasn't pride—that would come later. His first emotion was fear, the image of the ferocious, giant Ripper coming to his mind. Ripper wouldn't like being displaced. Not at all. Goblin seemed to know what he was thinking. "Don't worry, I'm not asking you to fight anyone today. You're not ready yet. And besides, we don't battle for position much anymore. Sharks die often enough without wasting lives."

"I—I don't know what to say," Gray stumbled over his words. "It's so ... umm ... weird."

"Weird to be appreciated?" Goblin nodded. "I get it. Sometimes when you grow up in a shiver where it's quiet, the sharks in the Line only see you as the pup they scared in the greenie for a joke that one time."

"Or when you got your head stuck in a bucket," Gray added.

"What's that now?" asked Goblin.

Gray coughed. "Nothing. You were saying?"

"What I see is a big fin with lots of potential. That's why you're going to the Tuna Run with me and the rest of the shiver."

"You mean it?" Gray fairly shouted. He was being invited as a *hunter*! His own shiver didn't even want him as a member. Or they hadn't, until. . . . Suddenly Gray could only think about his mother. Goblin saw his sadness and bumped him.

"None of that now," he told Gray. "You're going to the Tuna Run, pup. And if you find your family, they'll see what a great hunter you've become. But you need to practice first."

"Practice for the Tuna Run? How can you do that?"

Goblin just smiled his toothy smile. "You'll see."

CHAPTER 14

THE GAME WAS CALLED TUNA ROLL. "IT'S NOTHING like the actual Tuna Run, but it'll help you work on your quickness and side-to-side movement. That's a good thing to have at Tuna Run and anywhere else in the Big Blue," Goblin told Gray.

"Sounds like fun!" said Snork. The sawfish had regained some of his cheery nature since Gray saw him last.

Streak jabbed Ripper in the flank with her snout. "He'll be swimming the Sparkle Blue in the first five minutes of a real run."

"Yeah, he's chum," Ripper agreed in his gravelly voice.

"Quiet down, you two," Goblin told them. He explained the game, which actually seemed fairly simple. There were two teams of six, symbolizing a leader and their Five in the Line. Both teams faced the same way. Gray, Barkley, and the other former members of

Rogue Shiver were one team and hovered farther back. Goblin and his Line took their places closest to the starting end of the field of play.

Gray's team was about twenty good tail strokes, or a hundred yards, away from Goblin and near the end line of the field. He taught the landshark measuring system to Barkley, who found it to be both fascinating and useful. In the game, a single drove of exactly one hundred fish would try to zip by both teams. For every fish Goblin's group caught they received one point; any that Gray's team caught were worth two points, as the fish would have time to gain speed in the water between the two teams. Neither team could swim outside their own zone, marked by glowing lumos. "The object is to make quick decisions and catch some fish!"

"Wait, wait," said Barkley, looking absolutely confused. "Are you forcing some poor dwellers to play a *game* in which they get eaten?" This struck Goblin and his team as hilarious. They laughed so hard they could barely breathe. Striiker and Mari also chuckled. Snork joined in, too, but Gray was pretty sure the sawfish didn't know why he was laughing.

"Forcing them?" Thrash could barely speak he was laughing so hard. "He thinks we're forcing them!"

"Like he's going to catch one anyway!" yelled Streak. Barkley gave her a glare, and she burst into another giggle fit.

"Wisko! Get out here!" yelled Goblin. A fish that Gray

had never seen before streaked forward and stopped between the two groups. This fish knifed through the water with ease! It shined silver and was shaped like a long, thin spine with jagged fins pressed close to its body. "This is Wisko, the wahoo. She's been in charge of our Tuna Roll for the last three years."

"She *what*?" Barkley asked, now even more confused.

"Watchu want, Goblin pup?" Wisko danced in front of the great white, tapping him on his head with her tail. For some reason this didn't bother Goblin at all, and he playfully snapped at the fish. "What's the hold up? Wahoo! We going or what? Or you too turtle to play today? Wa-hoo!"

"The dogfish is afraid we're *forcing* you to Tuna Roll with us," Goblin said dryly.

"Who? Who said that? Him?" After Goblin nodded, Wisko jetted over to Barkley, hitting him in the face with a tremendous tail slap.

"Hey!" yelped Barkley. "I'm making sure you're not being abused! You obviously aren't a dumb grouping fish."

"We invented Tuna Roll, dog breath!" said Wisko. "We play by different rules than the rest of the dwellers in the Big Blue. Hey, did you know you're named after a dumb land animal called a *dog*, which eats its own poo?"

"We're *not* named after it," huffed Barkley. "It's named after us!"

"So you admit you eat your own poo? Ha ha!" said Wisko as she finned Barkley's snout with another blazing fast pass. "Wa-hoo!" Barkley got angry and darted after the wahoo, but never came close to catching her. She taunted him as he flailed about. "Over here! No, here! Too slow!"

"Only the fastest wahoo are chosen for the Tuna Roll by their leader—that's Wisko. It's a great honor for them to test themselves against us," Velenka told everyone. "They're actually faster than the tuna we'll hunt at the run."

"Waaay faster! Wa-hoo!" exclaimed Wisko, a flash of silver as she pirouetted in the water. "We are the fastest of the fast, the quickest of the quick! So quick, it'll make ya sick!" She flashed by Barkley again, making him duck. "We're also the best tasting fish in the sea, pups!"

Velenka continued, "Tonight we have to bring dinner to the wahoo who get by us. As you can see, they are insufferable winners. If they get eaten, that's also an honor. They call it the Way of the Wahoo." The mako rolled her eyes as if she didn't totally get the Way of the Wahoo either.

"Wa-hoo! It sure is!" Wisko told everyone. "Getting old and slow is no way to go! So we dancin' or what, sharkkind?"

All thoughts of how the wahoo might be mistreated went totally out of Barkley's mind. He stared menacingly at the fish. Well, as menacingly as Barkley could stare, which wasn't very. "Then I'd love to 'honor' you, Wisko."

This comment got the dogfish another slap on the snout. "You'll be feeding me tonight, dog breath! Wahoo!" The fish twisted and swam back to the starting line, moving to a quirky beat in the tides only she heard.

"That is one odd fish," Shell said.

"Odd or not, it's so on!" Barkley muttered to himself as he ground his teeth in annoyance.

"Ready!" yelled Goblin, and his entire team swum into a ragged formation. When he bellowed "SET!" the line moved into a perfect two-tiered V-formation with Streak and Churn hovering topside.

Gray's senses went into overdrive. He hadn't noticed before, but there were loads of dwellers around. Squid, eels, octopi, crabs, and other bottom dwellers gathered to watch near or on the craggy rock wall facing the field. Fish of all sorts and colors hovered with the tide; smallest in the front, largest in the back. There were even a few whales in the distance, although they'd need very good eyesight to see the game. All of this was interrupted by Goblin shouting, "ROLL!"

A hundred shining wahoo cried in unison, "WAHOO!" and accelerated past the start line the instant after Wisko snapped her tail as the signal to move. Goblin's team stayed in their formation until the last second, then blasted out every which way. Streak, a very fast blue shark, got one. All in all, only two or three wahoo were caught.

"Stay together until they're right on us, then break!" yelled Mari.

But Gray's team couldn't hold their formation like Goblin's, and the fish were past them in a fin flick. It would have been nice to know that teams did that before the game, he thought sourly. The wahoo easily avoided them. In fact Gray was pretty sure Wisko herself shouted "Wa-hoo!" into his ear and gave him a slap on the snout as she whizzed by. While the wahoo were amusing earlier when they were having fun with Barkley, now they were super annoying to Gray.

Goblin's team was in stitches, laughing so hard they had to call a time-out.

"Did you see the look on Gray's face?!" yelled Churn.

"Nothing compared to doggie!" agreed Streak, still gnashing her teeth from her meal.

Goblin and Velenka explained the rules more fully between rolls, which referred to the rounds of wahoo swimming through the field. There were ten rolls to a game, and each team got to be up front for five of them. "Ohh, you're taking too long," Goblin told everyone. "Now you're gonna get it."

Goblin pointed with his fin as Velenka added, "Tyro had an off day when he created the wahoo."

The ninety-seven wahoo who made it across the line in the first roll were still slapping fins with each other and hurling insults at the sharkkind. But when Wisko snapped her tail, they swam into a tight formation.

"WHO-ARE-WE?!" she shouted, each word more of an exclamation than a question. The entire formation of wahoo began doing the same slow fin moves: three strokes one way, then a tail clap with the wahoo on their left, then three strokes to the right and a tail clap to the nearest wahoo the other way. They moved together perfectly in this massed victory swim, and *sang* in time to their tail claps!

We are the wahoo, the speedy, speedy wahoo!

WA! HOO!

You are the drifters, the jelly, jelly, drifters!

SO! SLOW!

We are the wahoo, the speedy, speedy wahoo!

WA! HOO!

You are the drifters, the jelly, jelly, drifters!

SO! SLOW!

"What the heck are they doing?" Snork asked.

"Right now? Insulting us," snorted Striiker.

"Don't let it get to you," said Mari. "Huddle up!"

Mari tried to explain the strategy for the game, but Gray couldn't hear her at all. It turned out that the gathered dwellers were cheering as loud as they could for the wahoo! The entire bowl-shaped stadium was alive with their energy. A school of glowing lantern fish circled the edge and all the dwellers rose when they went by—even the bottom feeders who couldn't swim raised a claw or tentacle—which made it look like there was an undersea wave rolling around the edge of the field! And lumos of all sorts were blinking together forming pictures in the shape of a wahoo!

Shell nodded. "Yeah, the dwellers always root for the fish."

Tuna Roll was incredibly fun and exciting! How could anything else compare? After Gray caught his first wahoo, Tuna Roll immediately became his favorite thing ever. First, wahoo were delicious, just as Wisko said they would be. And second, after having been so embarrassed by the fish, it felt absolutely wonderful to catch one! The game ran for four more rolls, with Goblin's team in front. After taking a small break, they switched positions and went five rolls with Gray's team in front. At the end of all ten, whichever team had the highest total score won. And flip, Rogue was getting killed! The score was twenty-one to seven heading into the last roll. Goblin accounted for eight points on his own!

Cheers from the dwellers rose as Gray began what was called the "sound off." "Ready! Set! ROLL!" he shouted.

The wahoo streaked past their line with a swimming start. Wisko was playing again! She angled the cluster of a hundred wahoo to the right. Gray was at the *diamond head* of the formation—there were so

many cool terms in this game—and moved to inter-
cept. Wisko was the fastest of the wahoo and blew by
them. But the stragglers, if any fish so fast could be
deemed a straggler, were forced to change direction.
Striiker ate one wahoo in a single bite. Mari and Gray
each struck home as Barkley just missed. Both Goblin
and Ripper were successful, though, further increas-
ing their team's score. Gray's team lost but, wow, this
game was fun!

"What a beat down!" yelled Streak as Goblin and the
rest joined them.

"Ah, they didn't do too bad," commented Velenka.
"Especially with a rookie at diamond head." The mako
brushed her tail against Gray's flank, earning a scowl
from Mari.

Wisko led the other wahoo through a song that
started out sad but ended with a rousing chorus, com-
memorating the wahoo who were eaten during the
game. They finished by shouting, "On your way to the
Sparkle Blue! WA! HOO!" After the song ended, Wisko
brought all the remaining wahoo to Goblin. "Time for
the losers—that's you—to feed the winners—that's us. See
you at Slaggernack's."

"We'll be there," Goblin told her.

The rest of the wahoo swam by, bumping fins with
sharks who'd done well.

Wisko passed him and said, "Not bad for a pup."

Barkley hadn't caught a wahoo. Not even close. He wasn't feeling good about himself and began to swim away.

"Hey, dog breath," yelled Thrash. "Not so fast."

"What? It's over, right?" asked Barkley.

"Oh, you wish!" Streak told him.

CHAPTER 15

IF THE GAME WAS GREAT, THE CAMARADERIE after Tuna Roll was even better. Everyone gathered in a series of coral formations and caves called Slaggernacks a short swim off the East side of the home-waters, which was named after a giant crab who had lived years ago. His massive exoskeleton stood there on display as if guarding the place. Everyone who entered slapped a fin on Slaggernack's giant claw for luck before moving between jagged outcroppings of coral that were covered with glowing anemones and dwellers of all types. Even though the place was dark—with just a sliver moon above—and mostly enclosed by rock and greenie, lumos provided a great deal of their own light to brighten the place. There was also a small vent that blew warm water upward toward everyone's belly. Velenka said it was prehistore water from the Dark Blue that was warmed by volcanoes far below the ocean floor. It felt very pleasant.

Thrash explained that Slaggernacks was a free zone, meaning anyone could come, even competing shivers like Razor's, and there was absolutely no fighting allowed. "You mean if Goblin and Razor came in here at the same time, they wouldn't attack each other?" Gray asked.

"Nope. They wouldn't," the big tiger shark said before gulping down another seasoned halibut. Apparently you could get fish with mosses, planketon, krill, and other *seasonings*—a landshark word—made by the crab *chefs* here at Slaggernacks. That was one of the reasons the place was a gathering spot. Gray nearly threw up when he tried a piece. It was horrible! Whatever the shellheads put on the fish made him feel like something exploded inside his mouth. The flavor was everywhere—and strong! Thrash called it an acquired taste. Maybe it was, if by "acquired" he meant disgusting. The tiger motioned with a fin toward the urchins lying inside of Slaggernack's skeletal remains. "Those urchins are part of Gafin's crew. He owns the place.

"Gafin?"

Thrash shook his head. "I keep forgetting you're from the boonie-greenie." The tiger chuckled. "Gafin is the king of the urchins. He does business with lionfish, stonefish, scorpion fish, and any other poisonous dweller you've heard about. And a bunch you haven't."

"*King* of the urchins? Are you yanking my tail, Thrash?"

"No, I'm totally serious," the Tiger told him. "His territory actually covers most of the North Atlantis, including both Goblin and Razor shiver homewaters."

"Oh, so that's why Goblin and Razor can't fight here," Gray said, realizing this.

Thrash nodded. "Exactly. No one wants to be on Gafin's bad side. You can kill one urchin or stonefish. But sometime, somewhere, you *will* get stung." The tiger took a dainty bite from a seasoned fish and caught Gray chuckling. "You're supposed to *savor* the flavor, not just gulp it down like—oh, forget it. Fine dining is wasted on you."

Gray pointed a fin at the urchins clinging in and around Slaggernack's skeleton. "So, which one is Gafin?"

"I don't know. Go stick your snout in there if you wanna find out." Thrash called over a few spiny shrimp to drop the last small bit of his meal in his mouth and ordered another dish—haddock this time. Apparently the tiger would have to catch many fish, four to one, to pay for this meal. It was quite a deal for Gafin, king of the urchins. Before the spiny shrimp swam their way up to his mouth, Thrash told Gray, "By the way that's a joke. Don't stick your nose in Gafin's business. Ever."

Barkley, Snork, Shell, and Churn returned with fish for the wahoo. The losing team's three lowest point scorers and the low *roller* on the winning team were charged with getting the fish. It was called wahoo work. Gray had heard this term from sharkkind in Goblin Shiver but never knew what it meant until now. Wahoo work was any menial, embarrassing job. Ha!

The wahoo divided up the meal and took positions of honor above the sharks. They then proceeded to critique the two teams' performances in the Tuna Roll from best to worst. This they called rolling abuse. Not all of it was abuse.

"Still the baddest fin in Atlantis! Wa-hoo!" was how Wisko led off Goblin's rave review to the fin-slapping applause of the rest of the wahoo. Ripper, Velenka, and Streak were also praised. Thrash got angry at his so-so grading and needed calming by Goblin, who reminded him it was just a game. Churn received some razzing but took it in stride. The whitetip still scored more points than any of the Rogue team members besides Gray.

Wisko gave Gray a tail slap to the flank to begin his heckling. "Wide load here had the best showing by a rookie I've ever seen in my life! Wa-hoo!"

Gray wasn't sure he liked the "wide load" comment but knew it was said in a spirit of friendship, though Barkley was laughing a little more than necessary.

Another wahoo commented, "You've got yourself a keeper there, Goblin!"

Striiker and Mari were made fun of, but their performances were pretty good. Shell ate a wahoo during the roll, so even though he got an earful, he didn't mind.

"This sawfish bit me and *still* couldn't slow me down!" said another wahoo. "Laaaame!" He proudly showed a small divot taken out of his tail. Snork chuckled, a little embarrassed.

Gray was sure there were more comments to come about Snork, but Barkley interrupted. "Why don't you quit picking on him and shut up?" said the dogfish. Bad move. Everyone's attention turned completely to him.

"Look who suddenly got his big fins!" said Wisko. "Dog breath, the world's *worst* Tuna Roller!"

The rest of the wahoo joined in. "Bark for us, dog breath! That's what doggies do! Bark! Bark!" Soon the entire pack of fish were *barking*—they were making some kind of noise anyhow; Gray wasn't sure if it was actually how a landshark dog sounded or not.

"You're not even a real shark, doggie fish!" yelled another. And those were some of the nicer comments. It got worse when Thrash joined in.

"Maybe we should make him wear one of those, what is it—a *collar*—around his neck like those landshark things!" added the tiger very unhelpfully. "Wisko and the others can trade off on taking him for a swim!"

Goblin and his Line laughed right along with the wahoo. The rest of Rogue struggled not to laugh, except for Mari. She was genuinely upset at the treatment Barkley was receiving and glared at anyone from Rogue who was laughing.

Gray felt ashamed for his friend, but a chuckle escaped his teeth before he could stop it. It was an accident, but Barkley saw. The look in his eyes told Gray that he had totally betrayed him with that snicker. "You're a krill-faced whale!" the dogfish yelled, close to tears.

"Hey, you didn't mind laughing it up when they called me 'wide load'!" Gray was getting annoyed now. Barkley was always running his mouth about things he could do well at, like school, and making fun of others who weren't good at it. "You can fin it out but you sure can't take it, huh?"

Barkley rushed him. For a moment Gray thought he might take a chunk out of his side, but the dogfish whooshed out of Slaggernack's to the derisive hoots of Goblin Shiver. Led by Wisko, the wahoo sang a mocking song about dogfish. Gray later learned that they had a song about *everything*.

"You all suck algae!" Barkley yelled on his way out as the wahoo began barking a chorus in their song. Wow. Gray wanted to go after Barkley and make things better. He really did. To his mind, though, the dogfish was being thin-skinned again. How could anyone be angry here? This place was so cool!

But Gray decided to follow him, anyway. After all, Barkley was his friend. Gray was about to leave when

Goblin came over with Velenka. "Don't worry about your friend," the pretty mako told Gray. "Streak will teach him a couple of moves, and he'll catch a wahoo next time."

"Ripper used to be terrible, but now, watch out," Goblin said.

Gray considered. "I really should check up on him."

"Give him time to cool off," the great white told him. "You're just going to make it worse, and besides it'd be rude to leave so soon. Wisko named you rookie of the year!"

"Barkley will be fine," Velenka reassured him, her eyes hypnotizing him with their sheer blackness.

"Okay," agreed Gray. "You're right."

"Or he's not tough enough," Goblin mused. "And that's not your problem."

Gray disagreed and shook his snout side-to-side. "I'll help him toughen up."

Suddenly a peculiar wailing interrupted their conversation, and for a moment everyone stopped. "Oh, the entertainment's starting!" Velenka exclaimed.

An old gray whale and a few dolphins hovered on the edge of the cove. They were singing a strange yet uplifting song. "There's usually music after a Roll," Velenka explained. "We provide them with the entertainment of watching the game, and they do this for us in return."

Amazing! This day kept getting better and better. Gray knew he should go see if Barkley was all right.

And he would. In another hour or so. It would be rude to leave while the whales and dolphins were singing. He couldn't just take off. After all, he was rookie of the year!

Gray was so absorbed he didn't notice Mari motion to Striiker, Shell, and Snork. The former members of Rogue Shiver quietly slipped away, one by one.

THE
CURRENT
QUICKENS

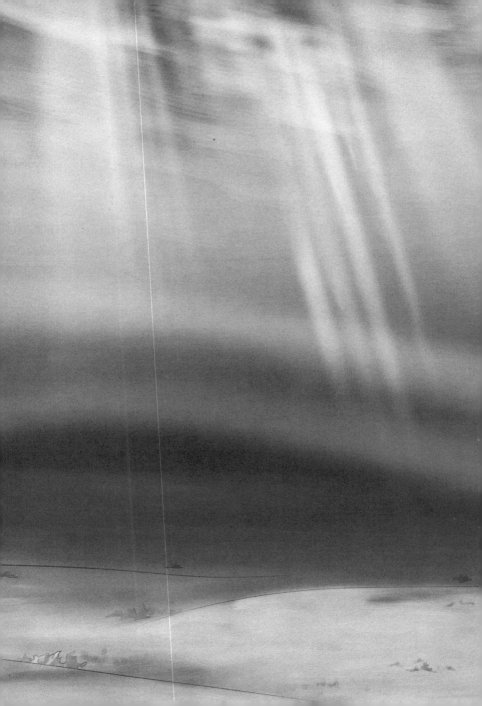

CHAPTER 16

BARKLEY CHURNED FURIOUSLY THROUGH THE dark waters. The homewaters of the Goblin Shiver, and more importantly, Slaggernacks Cove, were now behind him. "Stupid wahoo and their stupid game!" he muttered to himself. Barkley couldn't believe Gray had laughed with all the others. Sure, Gray was better than he was at Tuna Roll, but that was no reason to make fun of your best friend. I'll bet plenty sharks aren't good at it, he thought. Although, even Snork had gotten closer than he had to catching a wahoo. How could they be so fast? Oh, how Barkley would have loved to have seen the surprised look on Wisko's face if he'd caught her! "The honor is all mine," he'd tell her and then, crunch! Barkley shook his head. Keep dreaming, doggie breath.

He was wandering aimlessly when the others found him. Gray wasn't with them.

"Are you okay?" Mari asked, concerned.

"You kind of expect it from the wahoos; they're weird. But from your own shiver? That's cold," added Shell as Striiker nodded in agreement behind him.

Snork patted Barkley on the back with his fin. "Thanks for sticking up for me."

Barkley was so grateful for his new friends that he felt as though he was going to tear up. It was bad enough everyone saw him cry on his way out of Slaggernack's. "You guys are the best," he croaked, trying to make sure his voice didn't crack too much. "I wish we'd never been caught by Goblin. And not just because of today." Barkley sniffled. "I think it was much better when we were Rogue Shiver." Where was Gray? How could he not be here?

"You and me both, Barkley," said Striiker. "So what are we going to do about it?" He gave a pointed look at Mari.

"You're serious?" she asked. "Goblin will never let us leave."

"I'm not saying we should ask for permission," Striiker told the thresher. "Do you all still accept me as your leader?" Barkley didn't quite know what was going on. But if he was going to be led, he'd rather Striiker do it than Goblin.

They all nodded, Mari hesitantly. "Why are you asking?"

"I'll challenge him."

"Are you crazy?!" Snork blurted out.

Shell agreed. "Why are you so anxious to swim the Sparkle Blue?"

Striiker stubbornly whipped his tail back and forth. "I can take him."

Barkley shook his head. "Look, no one wants to leave more than me, but why fight at all? Why not just go?"

"Where?" Striiker asked. "The Sific? It's a long trip."

"And it could be worse than here," added Mari. "No, if we're going to do anything, we should go back to our old place at the landshark wreck. They don't know where it is."

"But," Shell said, "they'd find us." The group knew this was true. If they left the shiver without permission and were caught again, it would be certain death.

"Let's not do anything hasty," Barkley said. "No fighting. No leaving. Who knows, maybe Goblin will go to the Sparkle Blue at the Tuna Run."

"Now that's a thought," Striiker mused, a faraway look in his eyes.

Mari got in Striiker's face. "Don't do anything stupid! Do. Not." She stared at the great white until he nodded.

"Someone will have to stand up to Goblin one day," he told Mari. "We're just putting it off."

Barkley didn't want to fight the great white or his shiver. That wasn't the way to find his family, if they were still alive. It wasn't a way to remain alive, either. "Look, we all know I didn't eat during the game, so I'm going to take a swim and hunt," Barkley said. "Thanks for coming, all of you. I'll meet you later. You're good friends."

"Unlike Gray," Striiker said under his breath. But everyone heard. The four swam back to the Goblin Shiver homewaters.

A short time later Barkley spied a few fat mackerel feeding on sardines. He zoomed in and caught one, picturing Wisko instead. "Oh, please, Barkley, your teeth are so sharp!" he imagined the wahoo crying. That would serve her right. He pursued another mackerel into the low greenie but lost the fish.

Keep dreaming about catching a wahoo, dog breath, he told himslef. You can't even catch a stupid mackerel.

It was then he heard voices. Barkley moved forward slowly, not disturbing the sand or leaving a trail as he swam through the kelp bed. He peered through the feathery strands of blue and red greenie while hovering with the tide.

"You like how I piled on?" the voice asked. Barkley stalked forward to get a better look but remained well-hidden. It was Thrash.

Then a female voice sighed, irritated, "Fine, it was funny. But we have more important things to do."

"Like that little muck-sucker didn't deserve it!" Thrash huffed. "He's always looking down on me, like he thinks I'm stupid or something." Barkley's eyes popped open in surprise as he hadn't given Thrash credit for being smart enough to *know* he thought that. Apparently he was mistaken and had made a large tiger shark into an angry enemy.

"We have to get along for now," the female voice said. The tide pushed Barkley ever so slightly. Instead of correcting, he let it ease him sideways. This gave him a different angle which revealed—Velenka! The mako continued, "You can annoy his friends, but don't hurt them."

So the whole thing was a setup? Were the wahoo in on it, too? No, Barkley thought, he was just really bad at Tuna Roll. But what was the rest about?

"I don't know why we're going through all this trouble just to get some fat pup on our side," Thrash said. "I think we should just eat them instead."

"You're not supposed to *think* about anything; you do what I tell you to do!"

Barkley got very worried. The fat pup was Gray! Not that he was fat, of course—just big cartilaged. They were planning to use his friend in some scheme! He strained to listen as the tide shifted, carrying their voices away.

Thrash looked confused. "You mean I should do what *Goblin* tells *you* to tell *me* to do, right?"

The pretty mako became all sweetness and light. "Of course. And you're doing a great job. You'll be first in the Line for sure. But for now we've got to keep this a secret. So, did you pass the message to Kilo?"

"Yeah, I did. Streak would blow her top if she knew we were dealing with the bulls," he said. "This deal is rotten."

Velenka looked as if she wanted to eat the tiger's liver. She kept her temper under control, but her tail twitched with a lethal anger. "Don't talk about the deal, Thrash. Ever."

The tiger shark edged away. Even he was smart enough to be wary. "Sure, sure, Velenka. Whatever you say." The pair swam off in different directions, Thrash toward the homewaters and Velenka away from them.

What was Goblin up to? Was Velenka playing her own game? How was Gray involved? All of these questions and a dozen others rolled through Barkley's mind as he slowly made his way back into what he now considered an enemy camp.

"How did it go?" asked Goblin.

Velenka nodded, smiling as she swam over. "It's done."

They swam the open waters in silence for a while. The mako knew not to speak just now. Goblin was irritated, and when he was irritated, he was liable to lash out at anyone. "It feels like I'm betraying everything the shiver stands for," he said quietly. "My mother would have never have agreed to this. Neither would Hawley."

This needed to be handled gently. Ever since Hawley's

death, it was Velenka's duty to be Goblin's confidante. This was exactly the way she wanted it. Velenka was glad Hawley swam the Sparkle Blue. What would Goblin do if he ever found out that she had helped him get there?

A thrill ran down Velenka's spine at the thought of the thin current she was swimming. Everything was in her reach. Everything! "Your mother was a great shark," she began. "She led us well for years. And Hawley was a great friend."

"You got that right," Goblin replied.

Velenka stroked his back with her tail. "But times are different. You know that."

"Stupid landsharks and their giant nets," Goblin grumbled. "They sweep the Big Blue clear, and we're left to fight for scraps."

"And that's why what you're doing is right. You're leading us to victory." Velenka scraped against his flank the way he liked. "When the bulls are under your control, think how many more territories you can conquer!" Velenka saw that the thought appealed to him, but then his mood darkened once more.

"I'd rather it be a stand-up fight," Goblin told her.

Not this again! "We don't have the strength."

The big white whirled. "Then Razor and I, one-on-one, like the old days! There's honor in that!" Velenka was silent for a fin flick too long.

"You don't think I can beat him? Is that it?"

"Of course I do," she soothed. "But what if you were injured during your noble fight? What if he gets lucky and takes a piece of your tail?"

"I wouldn't be able to lead. Ripper or someone else would come at me for being weak," he agreed grudgingly.

"And your plans—who would see them through?" Velenka asked with all the sincerity she could muster. Pfah! She hated playing fawning fish to his "great leader." But for now, it had to be done.

"Many of them were your ideas, Velenka," he growled.

Did he suspect? No, this was a lucky strike. "I only agreed with what was on your mind, Goblin," she told him with a smile. "Can anyone really make you do something you don't want to?"

Now the great white laughed. "Not likely!"

The tension in her spine released with an almost audible whoosh in her ears. She could always count on Goblin's opinion of himself being very high. They swam onward, and she was forced to listen to him prattle on. For now.

CHAPTER 17

GRAY HEADED TOWARD THE AREA INSIDE THE homewaters where many of the shiver sharks slept. It had a nice current that allowed you to easily hover and doze. He felt guilty about having such a good time at Slaggernacks. He hadn't even seen Mari and the others leave. "What's so bad about the place, anyway?" he muttered.

Just then, Barkley streamed into view. Gray was glad for a chance to talk with him alone. It might get awkward after the dogfish rightly apologized for being such a little puffer. Barkley could be such an emotional shark.

"Gray! Gray!" he panted. "I'm so glad I found you."

"It's okay, Barkley," Gray told him. "I forgive you."

"What? You forgive me?" The dogfish slowed sharply. "*You* forgive *me* for being such a total flipper?"

"You weren't a *total* flipper."

"I'm not talking about me, jelly-brain!" the dogfish shouted.

Gray didn't say anything. He wasn't going to get into another fight with his friend tonight. Instead, he swam by without saying a word.

Barkley caught up with him. "Okay, we can figure out who was the bigger flipper later. I have something very important to tell you!"

Gray stopped. He was still miffed but would hear the dogfish out. "Go on."

The tone Gray used irritated Barkley for some reason, but he shook it off. "You're in danger! Goblin and Velenka are planning something."

"Planning what?"

"I don't know. She didn't come out and say it, but they want to use you somehow."

"She and Goblin?" Gray asked.

"No, she was talking to Thrash."

Gray looked at Barkley incredulously. "So now Goblin, Velenka, *and* Thrash are plotting against me? What about Ripper, Streak, and Churn? Won't they feel left out?"

"Please take this seriously, Gray! They're planning something that involves you, and it didn't sound good!" The dogfish hovered, gills pumping furiously, waiting for his reply. "Well?"

Gray shook his head. "Barkley, you sound like Yappy with his crazy stories."

The dogfish bumped him hard. "I'm trying to save your life!"

"It was only a game," Gray told him. "I can teach you."

Barkley swam in a furious circle, talking to himself. "Tyro's tail! He thinks this is about Tuna Roll! What am I going to do?"

"Calm down."

Barkley yelled toward the surface, "ARRGH!"

"What are you two doing?" asked Mari. "Half the homewaters can hear you." The rest of Rogue Shiver came through a nearby curtain of kelp, watching curiously.

Barkley told everyone, "While I was out hunting, I overheard Velenka and Thrash talking about some plan of Goblin's. It doesn't sound good."

Mari, Shell, and Striiker looked to Gray for an explanation. He shook his head and rolled his eyes. "I have no idea what he's talking about."

Snork finally said, "We're going to need more information, Barkley." The group gathered by a coral tower, instinctively moving behind it so they couldn't be seen from the homewaters.

"I know it's not much to go on," the dogfish began, lowering his voice for some reason. "But Velenka was talking about an alliance with the bulls. And Thrash didn't like that."

Shell looked dubious. "Goblin and the bulls? Unlikely."

"Could you have misunderstood?" Mari asked uncertainly.

Barkley shook his head. "No. And also, Gray's part of their plan. Somehow."

"Of course he is," Striiker said sarcastically. "He's the center of attention in *every* ocean."

"I am not!" Gray exclaimed. "This is all in Barkley's jelly head. If anything's in there at all! He's mad that Goblin and Thrash gave him a hard time. And what's so wrong with that, Barkley? I'm saying this as your friend, but you need a little toughening up."

For a moment it was so quiet that Gray could easily hear a single sardine swimming in the distance, its tiny flippers making a *switswitswit* sound as it passed.

Then the dogfish exploded, slapping his tail against the coral spire with a CRACK! "It's not about being tough!" he yelled. "It's about looking out for your friends!"

Striiker swam over to Barkley, getting his attention. "I'm sorry I have to ask this just to be sure—this has *nothing* to do with your really bad day at Tuna Roll?"

The dogfish gave Striiker a death stare and said nothing, though his gills pumped furiously. Barkley swam in front of Gray. "One more time—please believe me when I say that I'm trying to help you! Goblin has a plan and it involves you!"

"Of course I do!" Everyone spun around to see Goblin grinning, accompanied by Velenka. "I have a plan for all of you, and it involves being good members of this shiver."

"There, see?" Gray said to Barkley.

"What about the bulls? What about Gray?" the dogfish accused.

Velenka swam very close to Goblin, rubbing his flank. She spoke so low only he could hear. Though Goblin was perfectly motionless, it seemed as if he wanted to rush forward and swallow Barkley whole. "My plan with the bulls is to rip them to shreds," Goblin spit. "My plan for Gray is to let him help. Something wrong with that?"

"Unless you don't think you're up to it," Velenka remarked to Gray.

"I'm more than up to it!" Gray countered.

Goblin sighed. "If the rest of you want to leave, then go. I've got bigger fish to hunt." As if to prove his point, the great white snapped up an unlucky sea trout that swam a hair too close to his massive jaws.

Mari swam over to Velenka, eye to eye. "Just like that?"

"Just like that," Velenka told her. "You don't deserve to be a part of this shiver, you ungrateful turtle!" Finn rushed the mako, but Velenka did a nifty turn and slammed her in the side. "Like you could ever be my match!"

Striiker and Shell blocked Mari from making another sprint at Velenka.

"Go!" said Goblin in a commanding voice. "All of you leave this place. You can stay until we go to Tuna Run. If you're hunting in my territory after that, you'll swim the Sparkle Blue." Barkley stared at the great white, probably a little longer than he should have. "What, doggie? What now?"

"And Gray?" asked Barkley. "Can he leave with us, too?"

"Sure," Goblin told them. "None of you are worth the distractions you're causing."

Striiker looked very unsure of himself as he said, "Then, we'll do that." He, Snork, Mari, and Shell withdrew, swimming away from the Goblin Shiver homewaters, looking back from time to time. Almost automatically they headed in the direction of the land-shark wreck.

Gray felt torn. He didn't want to see his friends leave. "Mari, you really want to go?"

"I do."

Barkley stared straight at him. "Are you coming?"

Gray looked first at Goblin and Velenka, then at Barkley and the rest of Rogue Shiver.

"No. I'm staying."

CHAPTER 18

GOBLIN RIPPED AND TORE AT THE GREENIE, shredding the strands between his razor-sharp teeth and imagining the dogfish as his victim. But Barkley wouldn't go straight to the Sparkle Blue. Oh, no. Goblin would make sure his last moments alive were painful. Then he would eat every last morsel of the ungrateful little flipper.

"I want to kill them all!" Goblin yelled loudly. Velenka's eyes seemed to grow larger, if that were even possible. She had big eyes for a shark. It was part of her beauty, he supposed. They were well away from anyone who could hear, near a roaring volcanic vent, which added a constant hiss and rumble to the water. If you weren't directly in front of the shark you were talking to, your words were lost in the noise.

"How would that look to Kilo?" she yelled back, although not with anger, but just to be heard over the noise. Velenka knew better. The fish he chewed and spit out did nothing to relieve his temper and neither did the greenie.

"I've wanted to deal with Mari and Striiker since they ran away! And the others were feeding in my territory! *My* territory!" Goblin began taking massive hunks out of a hard coral bed, destroying an entire section. He might lose a few teeth but it made him feel better. "They'll swim free when we leave for Tuna Run! And they deserve to swim the Sparkle Blue!" he yelled.

"What if I could keep them from escaping?" Velenka mused. "Put them somewhere to wait for your justice?"

Goblin stopped. "'To wait for my justice.' I like the sound of that." If anyone could, Velenka would find some underhanded way to stop them. This wasn't how he'd normally deal with a problem; it wasn't in his nature to slink around like a mako, the sneakiest of sharks. He confronted problems head-on, with a snap of his powerful jaws. But they couldn't do that right now. Not in his shiver's weakened state. Not with Razor waiting to attack.

"What about Gray?" he asked. "Why are you so interested in keeping him in the shiver? He's just a pup."

"Exactly," she answered.

The vague response infuriated Goblin, but he wasn't about to let on he was bothered. Velenka constantly spoke in riddles and double-talk, never getting directly to the point unless forced. "So?"

"Have you been to the prehistore vault lately?" she asked.

"Not since I was a pup myself. Get on with it."

"You really should visit again," Velenka continued. "There's a legend among the mako about a shark who will unite the shivers of the Big Blue."

"Yeah, every sharkkind has a legend where they'll be the ones to end up on top," Goblin said dismissively. "Bunch of wishy-washy mush."

"That's mostly true," she agreed, "but in this case, *you* can be that shark."

He laughed, his anger momentarily subsiding. "That's crazy talk. After we get Razor's territory, maybe we'll conquer a few more. But the entire Big Blue? Impossible."

"Not for a great leader such as yourself." Velenka rubbed against him and whispered in his ear. "That is, a leader who has a megalodon in his Line and obeying his orders."

He chuckled. "That would be nice, Velenka. Now find me one."

"I already have," she said smugly. "His name is Gray."

Goblin was thinking of tail-slapping that smug smile off her face when he stopped cold. Velenka was right! The sameness of the teeth and the overall shape—how had he not noticed that? Goblin himself was huge for his kind, bigger than all but a few he'd ever met in the Big Blue. But the prehistore skeleton in the vault was gigantic! It could finish *him* in two bites, its mouth was that large. That's what Gray, the big reef shark *really* was—a megalodon! And the pup didn't even know it!

"With him in the Line, you'd be invincible," the mako whispered in his ear.

With a megalodon in his shiver—maybe as his first—Goblin *would* be unbeatable.

Goblin saw Velenka smile and something struck him as little off. He would have to swim carefully into this particular greenie.

Very carefully.

CHAPTER 19

GRAY LEFT SLAGGERNACKS AS THE SUN ROSE and shined into the Big Blue. He hadn't meant to be out so late, but patrol was boring with no sign of anything anywhere, and Thrash convinced him to stay. He and the tiger ended up having a great time, but now Gray was exhausted, having gotten no sleep. He and Thrash had spent countless hours flank to flank in the last few weeks. He could tell at first that the tiger wasn't too fond of him, and the feeling was mutual. He had attacked Gray when they'd first met, after all. But keeping up a dislike for one another was a miserable way to spend time. So, grudgingly, they began to talk and Gray grew used to most of Thrash's quirks and now thought the shark was all right. The tiger was kind of a braggart, and there was always some commotion when he was around, but Gray wasn't perfect, either.

"Ocean Spray really brought it tonight, eh?" Thrash said as he nudged Gray. Ocean Spray was a musical group consisting of a baby whale singer, two bottlenose dolphins backing him up, and an entire dance troupe of singing sea horses. They were pretty impressive. "That whale pup would make good eating, huh?"

"Isn't there a treaty with the whales to not do that?" Gray asked. The idea of feeding on the sweet-faced, adorable calf horrified Gray.

"Right, the treaty. How could I forget? I love the treaty!" Thrash said loudly as a group of dolphins passed. Then he lowered his voice to a whisper. "But if you're on deep patrol and find a lost pup? Well, the Big Blue can be a dangerous place."

Gray was okay with Thrash most of the time, but this was getting to be one of those times he wasn't. He yawned exaggeratedly. "I'm beat. Heading home now."

"Come on," Thrash prodded, "we aren't patrolling today. Let's get a bite."

Gray was hungry. And he didn't like sleeping with an empty stomach, which rumbled just thinking about food, in fact. Since Barkley and the rest of Rogue left Goblin Shiver over a month ago, he had grown longer by another foot at least, as well as gained a good deal of weight. I'm going to be the fattest shark ever, Gray thought. As if on cue, his stomach grumbled so loud even Thrash could hear it.

They went to an area by the North edge of the home-waters. There was a carpet of high greenie nicknamed Hydenseek. You could always find a snack at Hyden-seek if you nosed around a little. Today it didn't take long at all, and soon they were both satisfied.

"That was another good idea," Gray told the tiger as he playfully bumped flanks with him. "You're just full of them today."

Thrash swished a fin, signaling for quiet. "Look there," he whispered. They watched as a turtle led her young toward the greenie field.

"Hey, turtles aren't dumb fish. We can't eat them!" Gray said.

Thrash stared at him and snorted. "Says who?"

"You know. Everyone," Gray replied. "And we just ate, remember?"

"Things that talk get eaten all the time in the Big Blue, you know." Thrash took a couple of lazy tail strokes in the reptiles' direction. "Let's scare them."

Gray was uncomfortable. He liked turtles. The ones at the reef had always been polite and even nice to him. "I'm really tired, Thrash."

"Do what you want," said the tiger as he swam toward the turtles. "I'm going to have me some fun!"

Gray didn't want to leave Thrash alone with the tur-tles, although he didn't know what he'd do if the tiger wanted to do more than scare them. He reluctantly fol-lowed. The female turtle—the mother, as the hatchlings were undoubtedly hers—had no chance of escaping. She motioned for her young to head into the greenie. Gray could hear her voice pitch into a squeak, crying, "Swim and hide! Swim and hide, children!" But the hatchlings were so scared, they just crowded closer to their mother.

Thrash glided after her slowly, but still much faster than the turtle could manage, and said things like, "I'm in the mood for turtle pups!" and "Here comes a big, bad shaaark!" He lazily slid with the current so he was now facing the turtles and blocking them from the safety of the greenie. He gnashed his teeth together. "Just swim inside! You won't feel a thing!" Thrash laughed; a deep, mocking rumble.

The mother turtle panicked and began screaming, "Heeeelllp! Someone help me!" She was surprisingly loud for such a small dweller. This scared the hatchlings so much that they froze and echoed the mother, screaming the same thing, "Heeeelllp! Someone help me!" in their own tiny voices.

The tiger laughed at the turtle family's distress. He looked over at Gray. "You just going to hover there like a bump on a reef? Get in here and have some fun!"

"I, umm, you seem to have it, umm, covered."

Thrash shook his head. "You're soft! I always knew you weren't as tough as you acted!"

"I am too! I am!" Gray protested.

The tiger laughed, this time at Gray. "Well, I don't see you doing anything to show it."

"Please let us go!" shrieked the mother turtle as her scared hatchlings hovered behind her tail.

The wailing of the turtles, the uncomfortable feeling in the pit of his stomach, the lack of sleep, and above it all, Thrash's laughing, pressed against Gray, somehow inside his head. He needed to make it stop.

"I'll show you who's tough!" Gray streaked forward.

He blazed past Thrash and scooped every turtle hatchling into his mouth. He would have gotten the mother too, but Thrash's bulk blocked him just enough.

"Now that's more like it!" yelled the tiger. "How's the shellback today?"

Gray slung himself down in the greenie. Using the sandy bottom he skidded to a halt, ejecting the hatchlings from his mouth. Luckily, they were so shocked at still being alive they stayed mute. "Shhh, be quiet or I'll eat you for real!" Gray hissed to the little turtles before turning to Thrash. "Yuck, they were awful! All shell, no meat. I'd find a fat fish if I was you."

"Suppose you're right, but I can't let you be tougher than me, hatchling-eater!" Thrash laughed and then opened his mouth to bite the momma turtle in half with his jagged teeth. She screeched in fear, a cry somehow even higher pitched than before and so piteous it broke Gray's heart. He was about to say something when—

"Tiger, tiger, full of spite. Tiger, tiger, not so bright."

Thrash whirled and shouted, "Who said that?" Gray

also turned toward the voice but saw nothing. Apparently Thrash knew this insult and didn't like it one bit. "Come on out! I'll show you who's not bright!"

Now the voice came again. It spoke with an odd lilt like nothing Gray had heard before. "But I'm right before you, silly tiger!" And it was! There, in front of Thrash's snout, floated one of the oddest fish Gray had ever seen.

It ruffled its frilly fins and announced, "My name is Takiza and I do not suffer fools. So you, sir, would be wise to move along."

CHAPTER 20

GRAY'S MOUTH HUNG OPEN IN DISBELIEF. *Takiza was real?* Impossible! Gray didn't know what was going to happen next, but he wouldn't have missed this for all the tuna in the Big Blue! Takiza, if this was really Takiza—it couldn't be!—wasn't running from Thrash. Exactly the opposite! He was preening, right in front of the giant tiger shark! Takiza's huge, delicate fins were bright red and white, fluttering like greenie in the tide. How could this fish even swim with fins that looked so fragile—as if they could be ripped from its tiny body by a strong current? They were so frilly!

For some reason Gray remembered one of Miss Lamprey's lessons about the landshark world. There was an animal called a *peacock* that supposedly strutted around in ritual dances, showing off its bright, long feathers. This fish, whatever it was, was definitely the ocean version of that animal.

Thrash took one look and roared with laughter. "Did

you hear this flipper? He thinks he's Takiza! Looks like a piece of greenie I got stuck between my teeth!" Gray chuckled at the comment. It was kind of funny.

"You have the manners of a blob fish, and you smell like algae on the seashore!" This caused Thrash to have another fit of laughter. Gray too, truth be told. And the funny, ruffled fish wasn't done. "You will leave this area now. Be on your way, and perhaps I won't give you the beating you so richly deserve!"

Gray was sure the female turtle and her hatchlings were safely hidden in the kelp and wouldn't be found. But there was absolutely nothing he could say to stop Thrash from sending this crazy fish to the Sparkle Blue. That jelly had already drifted away with the current.

"How is it that tigers are always such unthinking brutes?" Takiza asked. "If your elders would spend more time learning how to be vital dwellers of the Big Blue, instead of muscle-headed bullies, the seven seas would be much more harmonious."

Thrash nodded, as if taking the fish's words seriously, moving closer and closer. "Wow, you're right. I should give that some thought. The next time I'm at a meeting with the elders, I'll be sure and bring that to their—" Quicker than a sea snake, the tiger lunged at Takiza and his teeth smashed together onto the fish. "Ha!" exclaimed Thrash proudly, "how do you like me now, *Takiza*?" The tiger began doing a little shimmy that made Gray chuckle. But then—

"Whether you are dumber or *slower* is a question to

baffle the wisest in the Big Blue." The frilly fish was now hovering over Thrash's head, but directly between his eyes where the tiger couldn't see him.

"Wazzit?! Where is he? Where?"

Gray couldn't help but snort in surprise. "Right over your head!" Thrash moved one way and then the other, but the odd fish moved *perfectly* with him! It was the most amazing display of swimming ever. "Still there," Gray told the tiger.

"Are you yanking my tail?" asked Thrash.

"I'm not," Gray told him. "He's right over your head."

Thrash quickly barrel-rolled, trying to get a look. Still, without seeming to put forth any effort at all, the fish that called himself Takiza stayed between Thrash's eyes, just over his head! Gray's mouth opened in disbelief. It was impossible!

"He can't be still there!" yelled Thrash. "And if you're joking with me, pup—"

Gray could only shake his head and gesture with a fin as Takiza swam slightly away so that he came into Thrash's view, but upside down, so that he was eye to eye with the tiger. Or rather Tazika, being much smaller, stared with one into of Thrash's much larger eyes.

"Is it your first day with those clumsy fins?" asked the fish calmly. "I've seen starfish missing legs swim better than you do." Thrash's mouth opened in shock as Takiza continued, "And to have poor eyesight as well? It seems you have received none of Ramtail's gifts. Are you sure you're a tiger shark at all?"

Then the little fish caught Thrash by the tip of his tail with its frilly fins and somehow swung him in circles! And fast! It was unbelievable! All the tiger could do was let out a high-pitched scream as he was whipped through the water. The little fish then threw Thrash into the distance, several body lengths away. "A wise dweller knows when he's outclassed. I give you the chance to exhibit wisdom and leave this instant."

Thrash got his fins underneath him. "I don't know what just happened, but you're going to be chowder! You hear me? Chowder!"

Gray was pretty sure that asking Thrash if he needed any help fighting the little fish would get him bitten, so he stayed quiet. The frilly sea peacock didn't, however. "Unfortunately I do," he answered. "Your voice is like the baying of an injured sea cow and hurts my ears."

Thrash was so angry he couldn't even respond in words. He trembled with rage and shouted an unintelligible "Gonnakillyerraggh!" before charging. The laughably small fish stayed where it was until the tiger opened his mouth to swallow him whole.

And then ... *something* happened.

Gray wasn't really sure what, it happened so fast. He caught just the briefest flash of the colorful fish zipping forward and snapping a ruffled fin into Thrash's flank. The tiger grew quiet, still moving, but not swimming—his enraged features frozen.

Then, he started to sink!

Gray swam over to him, concerned. "Thrash! Thrash?" he yelled. "You okay?" But the tiger didn't answer.

"The oaf will be fine after a few moments," said the little fish, now hovering in front of Gray's left eye. "I am a practitioner of the noble art of Shar-kata, a peaceful form of self-defense, which does not send anyone to the Sparkle Blue so lightly." Gray struggled to keep Thrash from sinking, but it wasn't easy to remain underneath him.

"Who are you? Really?" Gray asked, amazed.

"Excellent! You have manners enough to ask for an introduction," the fish told him. "I am a Siamese fighting fish, or betta." His frilly fins caught the tide and expanded to their full length. "My given name is Takiza Jaelynn Betta vam Delacrest Waveland ka Boom Boom." The fish gave Gray a flowery nod. "You may call me Takiza for short."

For a minute Gray didn't know what to do. He looked at Thrash, who stirred and mumbled, "Ma, is that you? Don't wanna go to class." Gray let the tiger settle into the sand and greenie.

"You're actually Takiza? You're real?"

Takiza moved his fins in another flourish. "I am."

"You know, I should eat you for doing this to my friend," Gray told the betta.

"You may try. But is he really your friend?"

"What? Of course he's my friend," Gray sputtered.

"He is an evil shark," Takiza said matter-of-factly. "Perhaps you should find better friends. Now, may I ask a question of you?"

"I guess so."

"Do you know yourself?" The little betta cocked his head and waited for an answer.

"I don't understand."

"Inside you, I see a shark who swims with one fin in the light and the other in darkness. Peace or anger? Only you can decide the current you shall swim, so which will it be?"

Gray couldn't for the life of him figure out what the betta was talking about. "What does that even mean?"

"If you do not know the answer then that *is* the answer for now." The betta shook his delicate fins and swam off. "Perhaps we shall speak again." And with that Takiza disappeared into the Big Blue.

Thrash twitched, sending a cloud of sand blooming off the seabed. "Huh? What happened?" He swam up to Gray. "Where is that little piece of krill?"

"Umm, you scared him off," Gray answered. He was pretty sure the tiger wouldn't want the exact truth. Thrash seemed dazed, as though he didn't remember everything.

"I sure showed him, didn't I?"

Gray nodded. "Yeah, that was...something, all right."

After Thrash gathered his senses, the two of them swam back to the shiver homewaters. Gray was dead tired when he got to the resting area, but couldn't sleep a wink.

All he could think about was Takiza Jaelynn Betta vam Delacrest Waveland ka Boom Boom.

BLOOD IN THE WATER

CHAPTER 21

GRAY SWAM ANOTHER MOON PATROL ON THE East side of shiver territory with Goblin, Ripper, and Churn. It was his fifth patrol in force this week, which meant that the group consisted of at least five sharkkind. Velenka, Thrash, and Streak led another down the Western ridge. The homewaters were tense these days as Razor Shiver sharks were spotted close by several times.

Goblin was also taking an increased interest in Gray, even scheduling one-on-one combat lessons. It was so much more than just ramming and biting! Strength and size were important, but real fighting was about tactics. What to do in a given battle depended on the particulars of the situation. Were you fighting alone or with other sharks? Were the numbers in your favor? Did you have the element of surprise? Were you swimming with or against the current? It was how you answered these questions, and many others, that would prove if you were a true mariner, or just another brawling sharkkind.

Goblin said that in the old days of the empire, some sharkkind battles involved armadas of sharks and dwellers that fought in formation, with the opposing forces clashing at different points on what they called the *battle waters*. Apparently humans did the same thing when fighting on land and in their ships on top of the ocean. Sharkkind had given the humans the idea of massed battle formations, but of course the landsharks said it was the other way around. As if . . .

In their last single-combat practice, Gray fought Goblin to a standstill. He thought the shiver leader was going to bite him in anger, but the great white laughed instead. "Now you're doing it!" he told Gray. "You're getting tough!" In the Big Blue that was the only way to survive.

But Gray had been troubled since his meeting with Takiza. A week had passed, and he still hadn't told anyone about it. Thrash was quiet about it too, but that was likely because he may have finally remembered the frilly fish beating the stuffing out of him. Somehow Gray knew the betta swam the Big Blue without concern, without constant fear or anger. What would it be like to live that way?

"You're quiet today," said Goblin. "Anything the matter?"

"Nothing," Gray began, but then he said, "You ever think if all the shivers stopped the patrols and stopped trying to take territory from each other that maybe things would be better?"

"You mean in a perfect ocean? Where there's enough food for everyone?" Goblin asked sarcastically. "Where magical sea horses pull us around so we don't have to swim?"

Gray nodded. "I guess you're right. Too good to be true, huh?"

"You know it. What brought this on?"

"I met this little fish, a betta, named—"

"Takiza." Goblin almost choked on the name. "The *peace-loving* Siamese fighting fish."

"You know him?" Gray asked, surprised.

"Don't know him, know *of* him," answered Goblin. "There are stories about Takiza all around the Big Blue. Crazy stuff about how he's invincible. He's more than five hundred years old—if you believe it." Goblin cast a sidelong glance toward him. "Did you fight him?"

"No, just talked," Gray said. He wouldn't tell Goblin about Thrash's beating. The great white would definitely make fun of the tiger and that would be trouble for everyone.

"Peace and love makes the current go around, eh?" The great white shook his head. "But that little flipper supposedly kicks some serious tail. So you tell me, why is such a nonviolent fish so good at fighting?"

"I'm not sure."

"Because he's not peace-loving," Goblin continued, "Why would you learn to fight so well if you
believed that peace and harmony is the way to go?
No, no, he learned how to fight so he can crush anyone he meets."

This was an excellent point. Why would a fish who
preached the evils of violence be so good at finning it out
himself? It should have stopped the nagging thoughts in
Gray's mind, but somehow made them worse.

Suddenly Churn cried, "Razor Shiver!"

Eight bull sharks were resting on the other side
of an immense field of glowing coral. The coral was
beautiful to Gray's eyes, different spires casting eerie
light everywhere: pink, red, blue, green, and yellow.
Everything was lit by the ethereal glow of moonlight
from above the chop-chop. But no one stopped to
admire this.

Without a word the bulls sped up, and the two shivers clashed over the shimmering coral field. Though
everything was in a frenzy of commotion, time slowed
for Gray. The cries of bloody victory and death receded
until he only heard his heartbeat and the water whisking past his gills. Gray rammed one attacking bull hard,
sending it spinning away just before it could bite Thrash.
In doing so, though, Gray dazed himself. His vision
blurred, and the rigid coral spires seemed to sway like
greenie in the tide.

"Thanks," Thrash mouthed. Maybe he said that aloud, even yelled it, but Gray didn't hear anything. The big tiger flashed away, avoiding a dorsal attack from another bull. Gray hovered and watched. Something crashed into him.

"Move it, pup!" Gray blinked at the shark in front of him, sensing that he should know who it was. There was a high-pitched whine filling Gray's ears, and whoever was speaking sounded very far away. "Can you hear me? Snap out of it!" The large great white whirled and slapped Gray across the face with his tail, and suddenly he could hear again. "STAY WITH ME IF YOU CAN!"

"Right, right!" Gray heard himself yelling over the sound and fury as everything came into deafening focus. Goblin battered a blue shark away from Churn, then bit the dorsal fin off another. Gray rammed his way through an attack. He knew his side should hurt, but it didn't right now. That shark was replaced by another, faster one. This bull did a series of tight turns, trying to get behind him, and succeeded in separating him from Goblin. Gray recognized this move, called the Sea Horse Circles. The tight, attacking maneuver could rip his tail off if it succeeded. To protect against this, Gray switched into Manta Ray Rising, a series of counter turns.

As he was swimming for his life, Gray caught only flashes of the continuing battle. Ripper took a massive chunk out of a bull, and a cloud of blood fogged everything, adding to the confusion. Churn was being attacked by two sharks and was trying to defend himself, but Gray couldn't get away to help the whitetip. If he stopped turning, he would lose his tail! Goblin narrowly avoided having his flank opened, then killed his attacker with a bite clean through its head.

Another bull streaked to join his shivermate behind Gray. Gray executed a violent downward power thrust to get out of the way, letting his second attacker accidentally ram his pursuer, who had almost closed to striking distance. In a moment they would turn and attack him from both sides at once and send Gray to the Sparkle Blue! There was no choice. Gray tore the flipper off the first bull, sending him spiraling to the bottom of the ocean, then charged the second bull. That attacker beat a hasty retreat now that it wasn't two against one, *and* Gray had the current flowing in his favor. Then, as fast as the battle had begun, it was over. The bulls were nowhere to be seen. All that remained was a red haze, already thinning. Soon it would be as if nothing happened at all.

Ripper bumped him from behind and Gray nearly jumped out of his skin. "Nice work, fin," the hammerhead grunted. "Goblin, you okay?" he called over Gray's flank. Goblin was facing away from them and didn't turn. Both went to where the great white hovered. Blood bloomed in the water around him. Gray got worried. With that much blood gushing from his body, the great white would swim the Sparkle Blue in minutes. But it wasn't Goblin who was bleeding.

It was Churn.

The whitetip had received two massive bites, one in the side and one in the back. "Did—did we win?" he asked.

"Yeah," Goblin told him with sadness in his eyes. "We won." And with that Churn's gills stopped moving and he sank to the seabed.

Gray wanted to throw up. "This is winning?" he asked in a shaky voice.

Goblin turned, but not in anger. "Yes, and it's not pretty. If the bulls have their way, we'll all be just like that." The great white pointed a fin at Churn's carcass. "*That's* what Takiza's mumbo jumbo gets you! A place right next to Churn."

Gray looked at the unmoving whitetip lying on the coral. Already, crabs and small fish were gathering to eat.

CHAPTER 22

BARKLEY WAITED IN THE THICK BLUE-GREENIE for his prey. He'll never know what hit him, he thought. He was careful to let the target swim past his hiding place before rushing out to attack.

"Gotcha!" Barkley yelled as he scraped Striiker's flank, but not hard enough to cause a gash.

As the great white groused, Mari, Snork, and Shell joined them from where they had been watching. "Your angle was all wrong! You should strike a fin or the tail if you've got a chance like that."

The dogfish's flippers drooped. "Oh. That *would* have been better."

Mari gave him a playful slap with her tail. "But your stalking was excellent! You were so far into the greenie that I didn't see you at all."

"Yeah," said Snork. "You're really good at sneaking."

"Thanks. I think," replied Barkley.

Shell shook his head. "How can you deal with all that greenie? Being inside the thick stuff gives me the willies. Like it's going to strangle me."

"If you go slow it slides right by," Barkley told the bull. "Just don't charge through it and you'll be fine." Barkley felt a little better now. He definitely wasn't the toughest fin around, but with Rogue Shiver's help, he felt a little more at ease in the open waters of the Big Blue.

They were practicing—Striiker refused to call it playing—for when trouble came. The great white was sure it was on the way and only a matter of time before it would show up. He didn't trust Goblin any further than he could drag him onto shore. Barkley hoped Striiker was wrong, but practicing was a wise precaution. Still it would take a long time, if ever, to change Barkley into a relentless, steely-eyed mariner.

It was just like old times after they got back to the landshark shipwreck. They were careful not to hunt anywhere near the patrolled areas of Goblin Shiver's territory. After the second close call, Barkley took it upon himself to monitor when and where the patrols went. Luckily, these were on a fairly regular schedule. Whoever was in charge of organizing the patrols, probably Ripper or Thrash, wasn't devoting enough thought to the task. Velenka definitely wasn't in charge. What was she planning? Barkley didn't have a clue what she was up to, and it worried him.

One time he caught sight of Gray patrolling with

Thrash. Obviously Barkley didn't pop out from his hiding spot to say hello because the big tiger was there. But he wondered whether he would have come out even if Gray had been alone. This made him sad. They had been such close friends. And now? Barkley wasn't so sure.

Striiker was muttering and looking at him. "Barkley, you've got to get better at this. If we get into trouble, we're going to need everyone." The young great white was always so serious!

"Why don't you leave him alone?" said Snork, coming to Barkley's defense. He and Snork were now fast friends. Barkley liked Mari, of course. Everyone did. And Shell seemed okay, but distant. Even Striiker, though annoying sometimes with his short temper, was a good fin. But Snork seemed like the brother Barkley had never had.

Striiker was about to start a full-blown argument when Mari stepped in. "He's getting better every day. We all are! And we have you to thank for that."

"I just hope there are enough days to practice before we leave for the Sific," he answered. "It's a long trip and there are plenty of territories to swim through."

"Or we could *sneak* through them. And Barkley's great at that!" Snork said proudly. "He'll be leading us forward some of the time, you'll see."

Before Striiker could get angry, Shell interrupted. "All this practice made me hungry. How about we hunt?"

Striiker looked Barkley's way. "Patrols?" he asked.

Barkley shook his head. "We should be clear on the

Western side of the wreck. But like you always say, let's be careful."

"Finally," the young great white said, "some sense." Striiker never could let anyone have the last word. Barkley wondered if this was a great white thing, or if all shiver leaders were like this.

The group swam to the area past the Western reaches of Goblin Shiver's homewaters. There was usually good hunting there, and this day looked to be no different. Though there weren't any large clusters or droves, the fish were plenty.

Barkley's stomach rumbled. He was about to launch himself toward his prey when Mari whispered an urgent "Wait!" She motioned into the distance with her snout.

For a moment Barkley didn't see anything, but suddenly a shark materialized in the distance. And then another, and another, and more and more. It wasn't a patrol in force like Goblin Shiver was using lately. This was different. There were pups and older sharks. Some were trailing streams of blood.

"So many," whispered Snork fearfully.

"I don't recognize anyone," Shell said in a low voice.

Striiker agreed. "It's not Goblin Shiver."

"Then who are they?" asked Barkley.

No matter what Striiker thought they should do, he always looked to Mari before deciding anything important. This was one of the things that, to Barkley, counted very much in his favor as Rogue Shiver's leader. Striiker knew Mari was smart, and even though he was bigger and tougher than she was, the great white valued her opinion.

Striiker looked at Mari now, and she said, "I think we should talk with them."

Striiker nodded in agreement. "Let's swim in slowly so we don't scare them into attacking."

"And what if they *do* attack?" asked Snork, his eyes very wide.

"Swim away if you can, fight if you have to. And don't head straight for the wreck, circle wide." All of this was very good advice. Striiker had his moments.

Barkley followed as Striiker and Shell took the lead. Mari formed a second level above them, with Snork protecting the pair's topside. As they rose from the greenie and revealed themselves, the ragged group stopped and quickly formed a defensive position with the more mature sharks on the outside. Barkley saw that these sharks were wounded. All of them. The pups in the group wailed from underneath their mothers' bellies as Rogue Shiver slowed to a stop, barely a few tail strokes away. Barkley was horrified to see that some of the *pups* were also injured!

A scarred, old thresher swam out in front of the pack. "We're not here for trouble," he said. "Just passing through. We won't hunt in your territory."

"That's fine," Striiker replied. "Can you tell us what happened?"

The thresher spoke in low tones to a couple of other sharks. He definitely looked like their leader and was probably consulting with what was left of his Line. He faced Striiker and said, "We're called Jetty Shiver. Our homewaters are about a day away in the direction we came from, a nice little reef." The thresher stopped, overcome for a moment, but the fin was a mariner and kept his emotions under control. "We were attacked by sharkkind from Goblin Shiver. We had heard of them but didn't think they'd come so far East. They took some of us to be recruits and killed others who said they wouldn't go. We're what's left."

Barkley felt sick to his stomach. Goblin was an evil shark!

"We're sorry for your losses," Snork said. The sawfish was tearing up. Strangely, this seemed to dispel any tension between the two groups. Snork was the best.

"You're sure it was Goblin Shiver?" Shell asked. "Maybe it was bull sharks from Razor Shiver?"

A small hammerhead answered, "No bull sharks were there. The leader of the raiders was a big tiger. A mean blue shark was giving orders, too. They said they were Goblin Shiver. Was it someone else?"

"No," Striiker told them. "That's Goblin Shiver."

Barkley nodded to himself. The tiger was Thrash and Streak was the blue.

"If you swim another quarter day to the West, you should be able to hunt there for the rest of the sun,"

Barkley told the thresher. "But Goblin Shiver will send a patrol through there by moonrise."

The thresher nodded. "We thank you and hope to repay the kindness." Their group began to move again. They could only swim as fast as their slowest member, though, so it wasn't very fast.

Barkley's mind raced. Was Gray with Ripper when they did this? Could *he* have been a part of the attack on Jetty Shiver? Attacking pups? No! Barkley could see that Mari was asking herself the same questions. He needed to know! "Excuse me!" he yelled to the thresher, who turned. Barkley's voice caught in his throat as he asked, "Was there a big, young pup with them? Kinda like a reef shark, but not?"

The thresher shook his head. "Nothing like that." And then the group swam onward. No one spoke as the refugees receded into the Big Blue.

"At least it wasn't Gray," Barkley told Mari.

Striiker got furious! "'At least it wasn't Gray'? I got news for you, dogfish! He's a member of Goblin Shiver! He's probably okay with what happened!"

"Striiker, you're not being fair!" Mari protested.

"Maybe he was there and they didn't see him!" the great white continued. "Maybe he was busy gutting some-one's mother!"

Barkley had had enough. "Come on, Striiker! I don't know why you don't like Gray, but I can tell you he would not kill *anyone's* mother! Not possible!"

"You're right." Striiker calmed. "But are you absolutely sure he won't be part of the next raid on some poor shiver if Goblin orders it?" Striiker whirled and left everyone in his wake. Mari, Shell, and Snork slowly followed him toward the landshark wreck.

Barkley grew cold when he realized that deep down, he wasn't absolutely sure what Gray would actually do.

CHAPTER 23

GRAY WAS STUNNED. FOR A MOMENT HE couldn't speak at all. Velenka, Ripper, and Streak looked on from their favored positions above him and the other full members of the shiver not in the Line. Goblin wore an amused expression, hovering highest of all above the Speakers Rock.

"Snapper got your tongue, Gray?" the big great white joked. "You have to actually answer the call."

"Of course, I mean—yes!" Gray said loudly so everyone watching could hear. "I accept the position of fifth in the Line!"

Then there was whooping and hollering. Goblin came over and bumped him, then Ripper, and then Thrash. Gray lost track after that as *everyone* was bumping and finning him. It was all in good sport, though. Moments before Gray's appointment, Velenka had received the same treatment when she ascended to fourth in the Line.

Later Gray found out that in the old days sharkkind actually drew blood in this part of the ceremony by biting the newly ranked shark, becoming family in the tasting of their blood. But there were times that the celebration got out of hand, and the promoted shark died from his wounds, so the practice was wisely stopped.

Gray couldn't believe it when Goblin offered him fifth! He didn't have a clue that it was about to happen. Everyone was congratulating Velenka—he was right next to her—and Goblin said in a loud voice from his position above Speakers Rock, "I now name Gray as my fifth. Does any full member want to contest my decision and fight him in mortal combat for the right to his rank?" Gray didn't want to be in the Line if it meant fighting, especially when there were so many sharkkind who had been members for so much longer. He was about to open his mouth when Velenka stopped him.

"It's just old-timey language," she told him. "No one will go against Goblin's wishes, and he wants you!" And she was right. After a bumping and jostling melee, the great white made introductions to everyone Gray hadn't met, and even a few important dwellers in the homewaters. Then the party began.

The celebration lasted all night long. A trio of whales sang songs while a school of lantern fish swam around the shiver area, brightening the place with their colored lights. Very festive! It felt good to flick his tail back and relax after the previous few days. Gray was still shaken by Churn's death and the ferocity of the fight against the bulls. True, Gray hadn't known Churn that long, but he had been a shivermate, and they had gone patrolling together once. Even though they hadn't said two words to each other, in Gray's mind, it still counted for something.

The weird thing was that Gray found something enticing about the battle after it was over. He'd felt horrible *right* afterward, of course. He'd sent a bull to the Sparkle Blue and watched Churn die. There was no way that wouldn't jolt even the toughest shark to his core. Gray had been so shaken, in fact, that he'd actually thrown up on the way home. Oddly, this broke the pall hanging over the survivors, who'd swam in silence until that point. Goblin and Ripper laughed, along with everyone else, and confessed that they did the same thing after their first battles.

The remarkable thing was that after the immediate, horrible blackness of terror and death subsided, there was something else. After you battled for your life—and won—it was incredible! He felt the bond he had with both Ripper and Goblin *change*. The huge hammerhead had pretty much been a rude and icy fish to Gray before that day. But since he and Rip (the hammerhead said to call him Rip!) had fought flank to flank, they talked often, Rip even divulging little secrets now and then. Who knew Rip had sea horse friends? Not that Gray was going to tell anyone about that. And Goblin? Gray would go into the blackness of the Dark Blue for Goblin. They were brothers now. They had fought together and survived.

And then to hear that Thrash's patrol was attacked by another shiver that same day! Thankfully they didn't lose anyone to this Jetty Shiver. Apparently their leader was so crazy that a bunch of their shark-kind decided to leave him and join Goblin Shiver. That was good! There was strength in numbers, just like the great white said. They would need every shark they could muster if they were going to avenge the death these bulls were causing.

Velenka glided over, her shapely form moving through the crowd like a sea wraith. "I need a little clear water," she told him, scraping against his flank. "Would the new fifth like to take a swim with the new fourth?" Her big, black eyes bored into him.

The mako occasionally made Gray nervous and this was one of those times. She seemed so sure of herself. He took a quick glance over at Goblin who was furiously pushing against Ripper in a test of strength. Whoever was moved over a glowing line of coral underneath them would lose. It was all in good fun, though. Goblin would probably get the best of the hammerhead, but not for a while.

"Sure," Gray told her. They swam from the raucous crowd. But Velenka didn't appear to be going for an aimless swim.

"Where are we going?" he asked.

"I want to show you something. Something special." The mako smiled and flicked her tail for him to follow.

They headed into a cave mouth. It was dark inside. "In there?"

Velenka chuckled. "You're not afraid, are you?"

Gray flicked his tail. "Of course not. I just don't want to get stuck." The cave looked creepy as all flip, but he wasn't a pup to be scared of the dark and followed her.

"Don't worry," Velenka answered. "It opens up into a cavern after a bit."

As soon as they entered the cave mouth, a few body lengths in, it was absolutely black. Luckily, Gray had a keen sense of direction, even though he couldn't see a thing. The water got much colder as they angled down, down, down. After a long stretch Gray thought he saw a faint, white glow. Were his eyes playing tricks on him? No, something was definitely glowing, and it was getting brighter. After another turn, it got *really* bright. Gray slowed to let his eyes adjust.

"Come on," Velenka prodded. "Just a little farther!"

Gray emerged from the tunnel into an underground cavern. It was immense. There was even a surface to the water above him, meaning there was an air pocket. How strange! The walls above and below the surface glowed pale white like the moon. Now that Gray's eyes had adjusted, he could see it wasn't algae or lumos, but the rock itself that was glowing.

"So, is it worth it?" Velenka asked as she flicked her fin at—

"Tyro's tail!" Gray gasped. "*What* is that?"

There, at the wall of the cave, half covered by rock sediment, was a giant skeleton of a shark. You could tell it was sharkkind from its curved, dagger teeth. But it was the size of a whale!

"We call this the prehistore cave," Velenka began. "This is a megalodon. They were the rulers of the Big Blue when the oceans were young. Some think that Tyro was a megalodon."

"No way!"

"It's true," she told him. "Why? What type of shark did you think he was?"

"Hmm, guess I never pictured him as anything. He's the first fish, so he's kind of like all fish, I suppose." Gray learned about prehistore sharkkind in Miss Lamprey's class. It was one of the few times he paid attention, because it was so cool. But she only described how they looked. It was one thing to be told that sharks were the size of whales but quite another to see it in real life! One time they took a class trip to a rock tower, where Miss Lamprey showed them a rib bone of something she said was a prehistore sea dragon. Yappy got really annoyed when Barkley said he thought it was just a whale rib. That trip was a disappointment. But this! This was incredible!

"It's huge!" Gray exclaimed. "What a monster!" He drifted over to the skeleton's rib cage. Gray could fit inside the beast's stomach with room to spare. He swam around the megalodon and stopped in front of its awe-inspiring jaws, frozen open as if striking at some other giant fish. Its teeth were at least three times the size of his own. "Wow. This is great." Some of the meg's skeletal teeth shined reflectively because of a silvery mineral coating. It was so smooth Gray could see himself, a rare occurrence. The last time he got a good look at himself was a year ago when he was near the surface of the water and the sun was shining at just the right angle. Today, however, he wasn't pleased with what he saw. "Flip, I'm really fat!" he whispered to himself.

"What did you say?" Velenka asked.

"Nothing, nothing." Gray looked deeply into the reflective surface of the petrified teeth. He smiled and gnashed his teeth, making a scary face into the silvered surface. He was pretty fierce, indeed. Gray looked closer as something caught his attention. His teeth were smaller than those of the giant prehistore skeleton, but they were shaped *exactly* the same. Exactly.

How could he have the same teeth—it was then he realized the truth. A cold prickle danced down his spine, and he unconsciously whispered, "I'm not a reef shark at all."

He turned to find Velenka staring at him, the blackness of her eyes like two holes in the ocean. "I don't think so, either," she said.

"You knew?"

"I suspected."

Gray shook his head from side to side. "No, it's impossible. Even I know these things lived a really long time ago!" he told her. "They're all swimming the Sparkle Blue."

"Yes," the mako said nonchalantly. "Except you."

"You're yanking my tail, right?" asked Gray. "This is some sort of new fin in the Line joke, right?"

"No," Velenka said matter-of-factly.

"How?" was all he could think to say.

"That I don't know."

What did this mean? How would others react? "It can't be! It just can't!"

Velenka swam over, scraping against him. "It'll be all right."

"I'm a monster!" Gray yelled. "How's that going to be all right?"

"Accept it. You're a megalodon, or at least a cousin of one. I think it's fantastic."

Gray looked at the meg's teeth again, hoping to see some difference he could point out to Velenka. But they were the same, which practically guaranteed that nothing in Gray's life would be the same after today. He wanted to scuttle underneath a rock like a crab. "I'm here to help you through this," Velenka said as she slid her tail underneath his belly.

"Thanks," he told the mako. His mind whirled. Why would his mother keep this from him? Is this why she never spoke of his father? Did she know? Maybe she didn't. But if so, where did he come from? How could it be possible?

A nagging feeling whirled inside his stomach when Velenka smiled at Gray. It was probably the combination of such a huge, life changing discovery and this creepy cavern.

Probably. But in any case, Gray was now much more worried than when he first swam inside.

CHAPTER 24

THE MESSAGE WAS MYSTERIOUS AND THE lionfish rude. Barkley was hiding in the thick greenie, watching the Goblin Shiver homewaters. The patrol routes and patterns had changed, and he was determined to make sure he knew the schedules. Even Goblin wasn't so thick as to not make a few adjustments after his attack on Jetty Shiver. Probably afraid someone will come looking for him, thought Barkley just before the arrival of his strange messenger.

"Hey, dogfish," the lionfish said after swimming around him once. "Your name Barkley?"

On the whole, lionfish were impressive fish, and this one was no different, having neat, two-toned brown stripes separated by white ones. Its fins were almost featherlike (he knew about feathers from seeing landshark birds hunt in the ocean) and stuck out everywhere in a dazzling display. But lionfish were also deadly, having poisonous spines in those feathery fins.

Barkley backed from the fish slowly, ready to streak away. "Maybe. Who wants to know?"

"I do. That's why I asked."

"Why don't you introduce yourself first?" Barkley said. This was a mistake.

The lionfish's spikes went rigid. He fluttered them menacingly and said, "That's on a need-to-know basis. AND YOU DON'T NEED TO KNOW!" He went on in a quieter tone. "What *I* need to know is, are you or are you not Barkley? And since I asked first . . . SPIT IT OUT!"

"Fine, yes, I'm Barkley."

"Good, because I was looking for you."

"Yeah, I figured as much."

The lionfish stretched his spiky fins menacingly before continuing. "I have a message for you from a shark, big fin who calls himself Gray." This definitely got Barkley's attention, and he swam closer to the lionfish.

"What did he say?"

"He wants to talk with you. And he wants you to ask everyone if he can come back."

"Gray said that?"

"Are you slow or something?" the lionfish asked. "I wouldn't say it IF HE DIDN'T TELL ME TO SAY IT! He says meet him by the half-moon rock North of the home-waters at high sun." The lionfish came closer to Barkley and whispered, "And he says to come alone."

And that was exactly how Barkley told the rest of Rogue Shiver.

"Never believe a lionfish," said Striiker. "Anything poisonous is a liar."

Snork nodded seriously. "I've heard that, too."

"Why would he lie?" asked Barkley. "Maybe Gray's in trouble."

"Goblin and the shiver will be leaving for the Tuna Run soon," commented Shell. "It would be a good time to sneak away. But why trust a lionfish with such an important message?"

Mari nodded and swished her tail in thought. "Did Gray use to talk with dwellers at your reef?"

"Yeah," Barkley told her. "Not a lot, but sometimes."

Striiker harrumphed. "If you ask me, I'd say he's been poisoned by Goblin first, and by the lionfish second. We can't trust him."

Barkley shook his head. Striiker had never been warm to Gray, but now it was even worse. Mari looked thoughtfully at the greenie swaying in the current. Barkley knew she was smart, so he asked her, "What do you think?"

"It's odd he told you to come alone," she said. "We should go with you in case it's a trap." Barkley didn't like not trusting Gray, but this seemed like a good precaution.

Striiker spun in a quick, angry circle. "Do not tell me you are actually thinking of going! It's too dangerous!"

"He was our friend," said Snork in a quiet voice, not wanting to anger Striiker.

"*Was* is the key word there!" yelled the great white. "I've never trusted him!"

Mari swished her tail in agitation. "And that's part of the problem! But if he's in trouble, shouldn't we help? Shouldn't we get him away from Goblin?"

Shell had been very undecided until this. Now he nodded to himself. "I'll go."

"Well, I won't!" shouted Striiker. "You guys go ahead and talk with that big, ungrateful flipper if you want! Not me!" And with that, he swam away.

Barkley and the others did go to the appointed place after the sun rose. He insisted on getting there early so they could pick a good spot to secretly survey the area. They saw nothing suspicious, so they went forward. The half-moon rock was so named because of its crescent-moon shape. The area surrounding the rock was flat, barren sand, with no greenie. And no place to hide.

Was Gray afraid that Striiker would attack him? Possibly, which didn't make Barkley feel any better about exposing himself and the rest of the group. But if there was a chance Gray was in trouble, Barkley owed it to his friend to show up.

The time of high sun came and went and shadows began to lengthen by the crescent-shaped rock. Barkley's spine tickled the way it did when he became anxious. He definitely didn't like being out in the open even though this area was beyond the patrol routes of Goblin Shiver.

"Maybe he's not coming," Mari said.

"Or couldn't get away without being seen?" added the sawfish in a whisper.

Both of those statements could be true. But waiting around any longer would be foolish. Barkley was about to say as much when he heard a voice come from behind the other side of the half-moon rock.

"What do we have here?"

Barkley grew cold. He knew that voice.

"A cluster of traitors!" said Thrash triumphantly as he glided from behind the wider edge of the rock formation. Streak and Ripper were with him.

It was a trap!

Streak's eyes blazed. "I hate traitors," the sleek blue shark growled. There was a meanness about her that Barkley had never liked. Ripper just grunted menacingly.

"Swim!" cried Mari. The group tried to dart away in different directions, but Shell bumped Snork, slowing them both down. Mari swam right into five more sharks from Goblin Shiver. Barkley turned in the direction they'd come from, but ten other sharkkind hemmed him in. Others were descending fast from above. There was nowhere to go!

Ripper barreled into Shell, knocking him senseless. Snork was so scared, he tried to burrow into the ground.

The shiver sharks all laughed as they rammed the sawfish.

"I'm going to enjoy this!" said Thrash, zooming toward Barkley.

Barkley didn't even feel the tiger's impact on his side. Suddenly he felt the water cool and sweet, and he was floating by the Coral Shiver reef.

"How did I get back *here*?" he wondered.

CHAPTER 25

GRAY FINISHED DOING DRILLS WITH HIS shivermates and was ravenously hungry again. Combat drills had been ramped up since their battle with the bull sharks, and everyone took their bumps and bruises willingly. Gray was bigger, faster, and stronger, but he was also becoming very good at fighting both alone and in tandem with others. Goblin supervised the drills while Thrash and Ripper led them. Gray could usually beat Thrash, but the massive hammerhead still gave him problems. Rip was smart when it came to fighting and owned a lifetime of battle scars to prove his experience. Because of the T-shape of his head, the hammerhead had no blind spots in his vision, so it was very hard to get after his tail or attack him from above.

Gray's ego wasn't getting too big, though. Streak fought with such ferocity that she beat him in a one-on-one battle. He thought that Thrash would laugh at him,

losing to the much smaller shark, but Streak had earned
the respect of everyone long ago. And the fact that she
also beat Thrash the same day certainly helped.

Gray enjoyed the battle drills, which kept his mind
off unwelcome thoughts and feelings. He now knew he
wasn't a reef shark and was actively hiding that. Where
did he come from? Did his mother know he wasn't a
reef shark? If so, why hadn't she told him? Gray missed
having Barkley and the rest of Rogue Shiver around.
Sometimes he was angry that his friends had chosen to
leave; other times ashamed he hadn't gone with them,
and still other times he was happy he had stayed. And
always there was the uncertainty and sadness about
not knowing if his mother were alive. Those thoughts
swam around inside his head and threatened to over-
whelm him.

Gray was just leaving the homewaters when Velenka
joined him. "You're getting very good," she said with a
toothy smile. "Thrash was really annoyed."

Gray grinned back. He had beaten the big tiger badly
today.

"Aside from getting my tail kicked by Streak, it was
okay," he said. "Who knew there was so much more to
fighting than ramming and biting?"

"Those are two very important parts, though." She
chuckled and nudged him in the direction of a secluded
area. It wasn't good territory for hunting, but he allowed
the mako to lead him. Sometimes Velenka seemed like

she genuinely cared about him. But other times it seemed like she was *studying* him. She thought it would be best to keep his secret about being a megalodon from everyone for now, which was actually a huge relief. Gray was still new to the shiver and getting his fins underneath him. He didn't need to be known as Gray the megalodon-monster freak while trying to earn the shiver's respect as their fifth in the Line.

"If you were a leader, what would you do?"

"Umm, I don't know." Gray was tired from the drills. And hungry. And Velenka was forcing him to answer questions when all he wanted was a nice, fat fish. "Help the shiver be the best shiver it can be?" There was a flash of irritation in the mako's eyes, but it was quickly replaced by a look of deep sadness. He couldn't help but ask, "What's the matter?"

"Have I ever told you how I joined the shiver?" She put an odd, distasteful emphasis on the word *joined*.

"No." Gray would have certainly remembered if she had. Now that he thought about it, Velenka never shared anything personal about her life with him.

"I was just a pup when Riptide Shiver came," she began. It seemed hard for her to go on, but she did. "Goblin's mother led, with him as first. It was one of their last long swims into the Sific, which is where I was born. They destroyed my home. They took me prisoner."

Gray tried to comfort her but couldn't think of anything to say. He hoped there was more to the story, but there wasn't. "I thought you liked Goblin. Liked the shiver," he sputtered. "How can you stand it?"

"That's what life in the Big Blue is about: choices," she said curtly. "I could choose to live or die."

"Why are you telling me this?"

Suddenly she was snout to snout with him. "Because you can change things!" she said with fervor in her eyes. "You could be the one to lead us into a new current, a new age!"

"Goblin is our leader!" Gray shot back without thinking. This felt all wrong! "You're his fourth! What are you talking about?"

The mako bumped him in the snout with steel in her eyes. "Under Goblin's leadership we've taken loss after loss! It's an endless cycle of death that won't stop until he's gone."

"Velenka, I lost my mother, my friends, and my home," Gray told her. "But you're not making sense. I'm not going to fight Goblin."

The mako sensed his agitation. Her eyes became calmer. She sighed. "Of course not," she told him. "Sending a leader to the Sparkle Blue to take his place would be wrong."

"That's more like it," Gray said. "Did you eat a bad fish or something?"

Velenka snapped her tail, slapping him in the belly hard. "No, I did not 'eat a bad fish'!" She calmed, again. "I'd like you to think about the future, Gray. Goblin will fight against Razor until one of them is dead. If he loses, can I count on you to step up and lead the shiver?"

"I don't know how to lead! Besides, Ripper is the first!"

The mako cut him off. "It's your destiny! Do you really want Ripper making decisions for everyone? He's strong, but stupid. I wouldn't put him in charge of a clam shell." Maybe she had a point. "Or Thrash? Or, Machiakelpi's fin, do you want to put Streak on the Speakers Rock?"

Gray nodded. Thrash would be worse than Ripper, much more unpredictable. And Streak seemed scared, somehow. Who knew what either would do if they were leader? "What about you, Velenka?" he asked. "You're the smartest fin I know. And you're tough!"

Now the mako smiled a smile that lit up the ocean around Gray. "Thanks for the compliment, but I like staying behind the scenes. A shiver leader needs to be imposing and strong. You're made for it!" Velenka scraped against his flank. "I suppose I could advise you, though." The light hit her black top half just so, and a rainbow rippled across her graceful form.

"Umm, *if* anything should happen to Goblin," Gray stammered. "If . . . " He looked around to make sure no one was hearing this very dangerous conversation. And no one was. Not even a single bottom-feeding dweller. It was odd. Absolutely nothing lived here. The entire area was a dead zone for some reason. They were in the perfect spot for the conversation to remain private.

Had Velenka planned this? Gray couldn't be sure, but it seemed possible. "But you'll be the first if I'm leading. That's unless Razor Shiver doesn't send me to the Sparkle Blue. Or Ripper, Thrash, or Streak. Or if something else doesn't kill me before that." Gray chuckled, bumping Velenka to join in his laughter, which she did eventually. "I'm hungry. Want to come along?"

The mako shook her head. "No, I have things to do." Velenka swam off. Gray sincerely hoped none of those things she had to do were related to this conversation. He wanted to make sure but found to his dismay she was already gone.

CHAPTER 26

IT WAS A PERFECT SUNNY MORNING IN THE WARM waters off the reef and there were fish everywhere! "What a great time to be a fin in the Big Blue!" Barkley exclaimed, the water whisking past his gills. Suddenly, there was Yappy, right in front of him. Oh, the little flipper was such a talker, but Barkley didn't even care! "Isn't it great to be alive?" he said to the sea dragon.

"Snap out of it, already!" Yappy yelled. Well, that was rude! And then the colorful sea dragon slapped Barkley in the face with his tail. And the slap was really hard! Much harder than Yappy's little tail should be able to deliver, anyway.

"Yappy, what are you doing?" he asked as the sea dragon began to fade away like a ghost. "Hey! Where are you going?" But the sea dragon was gone and the reef disappeared, too.

"Who the heck is Yappy?" Shell asked Snork as he

hovered nearby, a look of concern on his face. The bull slapped Barkley again with his tail.

"Okay, stop it," Mari told Shell. "He's awake."

"I think he deserves another couple whacks for getting us into this mess!"

Barkley wasn't at the reef at all. It all came rushing back to him. The ambush! The fight! And now they were—where?

"They put us in a cage!" said Snork before he could ask. Barkley looked around. It *was* a cage of sorts, made out of a whale skeleton attached to a coral reef. The ribs were the main bars, but razor-sharp coral grew between the large gaps, forming smaller ones. Even Yappy wouldn't have been able to wriggle through, although there was room for water to circulate so they could breath. No way the coral was accidental! It had been put there on purpose and then cemented in place to make the spaces between the whale ribs smaller. How would a shiver make a deal with crabs, mollusks, and whatever else, to do this? That was a question for another time. Right now they were prisoners.

"Is everyone okay?" Barkley asked.

"We've all got bumps and bruises, but nothing too bad," Mari answered. She hesitated for a moment, and then asked, "Do you think that Gray was a part of this?"

Barkley answered instinctively, "No."

Gray couldn't. He wouldn't!

Would he?

Mari saw the doubt on his face and got worried.

Snork trembled. "I'm scared." Barkley patted him on the flank but didn't say anything. He was scared, too.

"Okay, I'm getting us out of here!" Shell told everyone. The big bull furiously churned his tail back and forth to gain speed and rammed one of the smaller ribs of the cage. It did nothing except cause him to yelp "Oww!"

"Think you're going to bust your way out, eh?" came a voice from below. A lichen-covered rock separated from a wall to which the whale skeleton was anchored. But it wasn't a rock at all! It was some sort of fish that looked like a rock! It said, "Not likely. Not likely at all."

This scared the kelp out of Snork. "Talking rock! Talking rock!" he shouted, jamming himself behind everyone.

It was without a doubt the ugliest fish Barkley had ever seen in his young life. Did they live at the reef, too? If they had, he would never have noticed! The fish was dirty, with thin strands of moss and greenie waving from its mottled brownish hide. Its scales, if they could be called scales, were malformed; some bumpy, others wispy. It actually looked like something that swam the Sparkle Blue for a while and came back to life after not liking it. The entire group backed away from the fish, which was only as big as Shell's front flipper.

This was ridiculous. It was just a fish, after all.

Barkley swam forward and Shell shouted, "Watch it,

Barkley! That's a stonefish. It's the lionfish's uglier and even more poisonous cousin."

Stonefish? Well, the name was right on, Barkley mused.

The dweller took offense. "Who you calling ugly, krillface? I'll slice you good!"

"You're calling me krillface? I'll grind you up!" sputtered the bull.

"Just try it, bullhead!"

"No one is slicing or grinding anyone!" Mari said forcefully. "Let's all calm down." She introduced herself and the group, then asked the fish its name.

The stonefish used its stubby fins to flutter slowly in a circle. "Guess it don't matter much since we're all goners anyway. I'm Trank." He shook his head. "Youse fins got yourselves in way outta your depth, huh?" The stonefish spoke with a weird accent. "That Velenka's a piece o' work, eh?"

"What do you mean by that?" asked Barkley.

"Only Velenka and Goblin know about this cage," Trank told them. "And Goblin don't use the cage. Goblin eats youse if he's gotta problem with youse. He's a direct flipper, if youse know what I mean."

Even though the situation was dire, Barkley became a little happier. Gray didn't do it! It was the sneaky mako who was behind this. "Velenka! I knew it!" he said. "And how did you get in here?" Barkley asked Trank.

Trank hemmed and hawed. He didn't want to say

anything until Mari reminded him, "Like you said, it doesn't matter, right?"

The stonefish nodded. "I'm in here because I know too much," he said. "Gafin loaned me out on a job. I'm his best hitter, see?"

"What?" asked Barkley, not understanding.

Mari told him, "Trank's an assassin."

Barkley opened his mouth wide, but nothing came out. An assassin?

The stonefish laughed. "At least yer not all from the boonie-greenie. Anyway, she makes a deal with Gafin for me to do one thing, then changes her mind and wants me to take out the fifth in the Line, name of Hawley. Well, that's not how it works, and besides, Hawley was a good fin." Trank shook himself and a cloud of dirt fell away, floating down to the sand. "She put me here and got someone else to do the job instead."

Barkley's mind spun from the sheer deviousness of it. He had heard about the mysterious death of Hawley when he was in Goblin Shiver. Velenka got rid of Goblin's best friend and put herself in the Line to be his adviser! And now she was holding on to him and the rest of Rogue Shiver in case Gray didn't do whatever she wanted.

Trank continued, more to himself, "Gafin's gonna be one angry urchin if he ever finds out. Not that he'll get a chance, though. Once the Tuna Run's done, she'll kill him, too."

"What's happening at the Tuna Run?" Barkley asked.

"The Run is where *everything* is gonna go down! That's where she makes her move on both Goblin and Razor and takes everything for herself." Trank chuckled. "After that, youse, me, and every dweller she doesn't like is chum. Come to think of it, she and Gafin would make a nice couple, if youse know what I mean."

CHAPTER 27

GRAY GULPED DOWN THE LAST OF THE ALBACORE. He could have caught more but wasn't in the mood. This was one of the rare times he remembered not having an appetite. He swam farther out than normal to hunt, wanting to get away from the feverish preparations Goblin was making for the Tuna Run. They Tuna Rolled constantly, even in the dark of a moonless night, which made it much harder, but Gray was proud to catch more than his share.

After one game where he landed three wahoo in a single heat from the back half position, Wisko gave him such a joyous slap of celebration that he almost ate her in self-defense. Wahoo were strange fish. For some reason his conversations with Velenka and Takiza kept bumping around in his head, mixing together. Since the day Gray was banished from Coral Shiver, he'd felt adrift, cut off from family and home. What would he do with his life? What kind of shark would he become? That was the question that would be answered by his time in the open waters, in the wild Big Blue.

The current Velenka was asking him to swim seemed to be a dark one. There was something hidden in the mako's black eyes, and Gray couldn't figure out just what it was. But Velenka was a shivermate and the same couldn't be said of Takiza. Did Gray really owe the odd little betta anything? Takiza seemingly swam the Big Blue with no ties to anyone. No loyalty to any fin or dweller but himself. How could that be swimming a good current? Yet, the little fish fought a tiger shark to protect a family of turtles. Who else would do that? Gray grew hot with shame when he realized he wasn't sure he would have stopped Thrash. He'd tried to guide the situation, but there was no way he would have thrown away his relationship with a fellow shiver shark over a bunch of turtles.

"Did you do it?"

Gray turned around as the troubling thoughts thankfully slipped from his mind and Striiker slid into view around a patch of waving greenie.

For some reason Gray's heart leapt. It was Striiker! "Hi! Where's everyone else?" he asked.

"Like you don't know!" the great white seethed. "What did Goblin give you to betray us?"

Same old Striiker. Gray was in the mood to fight, but he realized it was his own thoughts and deeds that made him angry, not Striiker being his usual abrasive self. Gray wasn't going to compound the situation by doing something else to regret. He shook his head and swam away. "I don't have time for this. Say hi to everyone."

Luckily Gray didn't let Striiker out of his sight.

"Make time!" the great white yelled and charged straight at him!

Gray's training kicked in and he performed a half-circle dive, easily avoiding the rush. "Look, Striiker, I've got a lot of things on my mind! You don't want to make me angry!" If his goal was to calm the great white by saying this, Gray failed spectacularly.

"Oh, *I* don't want *you* to get angry, huh?" Striiker came after him even harder.

But Gray was bigger, faster, and better trained now. And he *did* want to fight. "Let's dance!" Gray had learned that the landsharks called single combat *dancing*, which was also a thing they did when they were happy and to attract mates. He liked the term, and Ripper and Streak, in particular, would always show their teeth in a wicked, toothy smile and say, "Let's dance," before single combat drills. It sent chills down your spine. Gray had started doing it too because he thought it was cool.

Gray rammed Striiker right in the gills with his snout. That'd teach him! Striiker slowed, wheezing, and hovered in a defensive position. "Why did you betray them?" he asked, gasping a bit. "They were your friends!"

"What are you talking about, jelly-brain?" Gray

shouted. "You came out of the greenie and attacked me for no reason! Where's everyone else? Where's Barkley? And Mari? Answer before I make you my lunch!" The last words leapt out of Gray's mouth before he realized it. He would *never* eat another shark.

Would he?

In any case, an uncomfortable silence descended. Striiker was definitely freaked out and seemed to grow less sure of himself. "They were ambushed coming to see you."

"WHAT?"

"A lionfish told Barkley that you wanted to come back to Rogue Shiver," Striiker said.

Gray shook his head in disbelief. "I don't know any lionfish! Are they okay?" The questions came out in a rush. Striiker told him the entire story. He even seemed a little ashamed that he hadn't gone with the group. He felt guilty that they had been ambushed, but not about not helping Gray. He went out of his way to make that clear. Same old Striiker.

Striiker told Gray about how he had searched for days and finally saw Streak going out from the homewaters alone. He followed the blue shark and found where the group was being held. "It's usually one from the Line and a couple of shiver sharks guarding the cage," he explained.

Gray was dazed. His shivermates were holding his friends captive. Could this be happening? "Maybe

Goblin doesn't know?" Gray asked.

"Oh, grow up!" Striiker yelled angrily, "Of course he knows!"

"But he gave his word!"

"His word means nothing! All he wants is power!" Striiker swished his tail furiously. "And he doesn't care who he has to hurt. Believe me. That's why Mari and I left in the first place."

"This can't be happening . . ." Gray whispered as his insides grew cold.

"I can't get them out of there alone," Striiker told him. The great white was absolutely pained by what he forced himself to say next: "Will you help me?"

"Of course!"

Striiker winced from his bruised gills but got in Gray's face. "But don't think this means we're best fins or anything. After we get them, we're going to the Sific. That's *my* plan. You do whatever you want. Like always."

Gray whirled and gave Striiker a tremendous tail slap to the face. Gray actually felt it all the way up his spine. "Keep running your mouth and see what happens, Striiker. And here's *my* plan: You show me where they are right now, or I'll beat the chowder out of you again."

The great white was shocked. Then slowly, he started swimming.

Though he didn't feel proud of it, Gray had finally gotten the last word with Striiker.

CHAPTER 28

GRAY PEERED THOUGH THE RED AND GOLD greenie as Striiker watched their tails. There they were! Barkley, Mari, Shell, and Snork! How could someone be so cruel as to jam them together like that? To lock them where they couldn't flex their fins properly? He grew angry. How could sharkkind treat other sharks this way? Or any dweller for that matter? This was wrong! Whatever loyalty he felt toward Goblin and his shiver was carried away by the current.

"The coast seems clear," Gray whispered, more to himself as he and Striiker hadn't exchanged a word during the swim over.

"Look again," Striiker replied, flicking a fin toward a rocky outcropping several lengths away from the cage. Sure enough, there was Thrash. He was talking with two more shiver sharks. Gray's emotions clashed. Thrash was a battle brother to Gray! How could he, of all fins, do this? And all the while the tiger had smiled and laughed with him when they were in the homewaters and on patrol. "We should go in hard and fast," Striiker said. "Scare them off."

Gray shook his head. "They may scatter at first, but they'll turn back in an attack formation." He couldn't see any way to get to the cage and free his friends without sending Thrash to the Sparkle Blue. And even now, Gray didn't want to do that. "Let me talk with him," he told Striiker.

"Look, I don't want to argue over who's leading who here, but are you out of your mind?"

"Maybe I am, but why don't you listen to me for a change?"

After Gray told Striiker what he was planning, the great white gave him a begrudging nod. "Nice plan," Striiker said as he went away, low, and in the greenie so as not to be seen. Gray waited for him to get into position and then simply swam into view.

To say Thrash was surprised was an understatement. "What the—Gray, hey, pal!" the tiger sputtered. "What are you doing here? I think Goblin needs you back at the homewaters."

Gray acted as surprised as he could. He didn't look at the cage, pretending not to see it. "I was chasing a lower drove of grouper but lost them. You see where they went?"

As Thrash was forming an answer, Striiker whizzed in from above and speared one of the two other shiver sharks in the side, sending it spinning to the sand. The other, a small mako, raced upward and out of sight.

Thrash knew he had been tricked and launched himself at Gray, who barely missed losing his left fin. He jammed Thrash as he passed flankside with his dorsal fin, raking the tiger. Both turned in counterpoint, but Gray was the quicker one. He could stun Thrash without killing him. Striiker was behind the tiger, blocking his escape angle.

Suddenly, Snork yelled from the cage, "Look out! Above you!"

Streaking back into the fight, the forgotten mako was now in perfect position to mortally wound Striiker. Gray gave up his attack on Thrash and used his speed to collide with the attacking shark, knocking it away just in time to save Striiker. Now Thrash turned. If it wasn't for Striiker slashing toward the fin to distract the attacking tiger, Gray would have been killed for sure.

With the great white now chasing Thrash's tail, Gray made a quick half loop to gather speed for the downward attack called Orca Bears Down and slammed into Thrash. Striiker was about to tear out Thrash's gills when Gray yelled, "Stop!" The great white crashed into the tiger but didn't bite him.

"You've made a big mistake!" shrieked Thrash, protecting his injured side. "Goblin will kill you all!"

"Like he wasn't planning to do that, anyway!" Striiker answered.

Gray shook his head sadly at the tiger. "Thrash, how could you do this?"

"NO! How could you betray us?" the tiger yelled. "I'm under orders! What's your excuse?"

"I'm not an evil shark, that's my excuse."

The other two shiver sharks got their fins under them and shakily joined Thrash. None was in any condition to fight, so they swam for the homewaters. "Tell Goblin I resign as his fifth," Gray said.

Thrash laughed as he left. "You can tell him yourself. Just before he guts you!"

Gray looked at Striiker, who gave him a bump on the flank with his fin. They had saved each other's lives in mortal combat. Like it or not, they were battle brothers now, and the great white knew it. Gray wanted to say something and so did Striiker, but neither could find the words. Then Barkley kind of ruined everything when he shouted, "Hey, I hate to interrupt your tender moment, but could you guys get us out of here?" Relieved from having to say anything, Gray and Striiker swam to the cage.

"I can't believe you just did that!" Mari exclaimed. "Goblin will explode like an underwater volcano!"

Shell looked at Striiker from inside the whalebone cage. "So do we like Gray again?"

Striiker told the group, "He didn't have anything to do with you guys being ambushed."

"Like I told youse," Trank said.

"Who's that?"

"That's Trank!" Snork explained.

That didn't really answer anything, but Gray was busy figuring out the locking device on the cage. It was cunningly made. You needed to disengage two bars that meshed perfectly together. Perhaps if Striiker or Gray had small fins they could have opened it by pressing down, but both were too big. And the area in front of the door had a pylon blocking the way. You couldn't take a swimming start to crash through it.

The great white figured the same thing and shook his head. "No way. Our fins are too big and those whale bones are too tough to ram through."

Gray got himself into a position hovering in front of the door. Striiker figured out what he thought Gray was about to do and said, "Did you hear me? You can't break those! Not enough room to speed up."

"I'm not going to ram it," Gray said. "I'm going to bite through."

"I'm pulling for you," Barkley said. "But are you sure that's a good idea?"

Gray got himself directly in front of the locking bars. "We'll see!" he said and then opened his mouth as wide as it would go. At first the petrified whalebone didn't give an inch. And for a heart-stopping second, he thought his jaws had locked in the painful position. Then his razor sharp teeth cut into the bars. With one last, loud, crunch! The door was ripped out.

After Gray spit the large bones out of his mouth, Striiker said, "Now *that* was impressive."

"It feels good to get some fresh water pumping through these gills!" said Barkley. He bumped Gray. "I knew you'd help us. I mean, I was pretty sure."

"Let's get swimming," Gray told the group. "Striiker said he knows the way to the Sific. That is, if you're okay with me coming along."

"Well, you're good in a fight, so that might be useful." And that was that. Gray was about to follow when he noticed the rest of the group wasn't moving.

Striiker got annoyed, of course. "You have to move your tails back and forth if you want to go forward," he sarcastically told them.

"We can't leave," Barkley said.

The great white sighed. "Why?" Striiker flexed his flippers as if he'd like nothing better than to ram Barkley.

"I'll let Trank tell you," the dogfish said. "Trank?" But the stonefish was nowhere to be seen. So Barkley and Mari explained everything they'd heard from him. When they were finished, there wasn't a doubt in any-one's mind where they were going.

Rogue Shiver was going to the Tuna Run.

CHAPTER 29

THE FINAL PREPARATIONS FOR THE TUNA RUN were being made when Velenka returned from her meeting with Kilo and his most trusted bull sharks. Goblin thought she went to make sure everything go as planned. Well, all would go as planned all right. Just not *his* plan, Velenka thought. *Mine.*

After sending Razor to the Sparkle Blue, Kilo and his followers would then turn on Goblin. Ripper and Thrash would be dealt with also. She had convinced Streak to join her, and the blue would help in the fight if needed. Kilo thought he would be Valenka's first, but he too was in for a surprise. A giant megalodon of a surprise! If she could just control Gray, and making him her first was her preferred way of doing this, she would be fine. But if Gray placed a fin out of line, he'd swim the Sparkle Blue with the others! Velenka would combine both Razor and Goblin shivers into a new, improved Riptide Shiver. She wouldn't be merely a shiver leader, but queen of the entire North Atlantis!

Velenka was so excited that she could hardly keep a toothy smile from stretching across her lips. Her plan was a thing of beauty. Machiakelpi himself would be proud! Unfortunately, she hadn't noticed when the bruised Thrash swam into the homewaters and began blubbering to Goblin until it was too late.

"WHAT?!" Goblin roared, which got Velenka's attention. She swam over as fast as possible. Ripper and Streak were already there. They were all in uproar but none more so than Goblin. "I'll eat them all!"

"What's going on?" she yelled, trying to get the furious great white to focus on her.

"I'll deal with them if it's the last thing I do!" Goblin shouted.

Velenka looked around for answers and noticed that Thrash looked battered as if from a recent fight. She went cold even before he spoke to her. "Gray jumped us. He freed the Rogue flippers."

"I told you we should have killed them!" Goblin yelled at her. "This was your idea!"

Of course it was her idea. Everything was her idea! But now Gray was a liability. Her plan could still work, but she'd have to deal with Kilo on her own. Velenka couldn't show weakness in front of Goblin, especially when everyone she would eventually rule over was watching. No one would follow a turtle.

Velenka steeled herself and looked Goblin right in the eyes. "This changes nothing!" she said. "Nothing!" She swam up close to—but not on—the Speakers Rock. "Everything you planned is finally in place! It would be nice to deal with those traitors, but if they run, which they most likely will, they're still gone for good."

Goblin calmed. "And if they show up at the Tuna Run looking for their families?"

"Or trouble?" added Thrash.

"Then you eat them," Velenka told the huge great white coldly. "But focus on what's important and get that done first. We're—I mean, *you're* so close!"

Goblin nodded, then yelled at the sharks who were watching and listening, "What are you looking at? Get ready to swim for the Tuna Run!" Activity started up immediately, no one wanting to arouse the shiver leader's temper by being anywhere near him. Goblin took out his temper on Thrash with a tremendous tail slap to the head. "And you! You're demoted to fifth! Ripper, Streak—come with me!" Streak gave Velenka a subtle nod and swam away with the others. But before they left, Goblin told her in a low, menacing tone, "When this is over, you and I will talk."

Velenka exhaled. She was in control of the situation. Everything was still moving forward with the current. Slowly, the warm excited feeling in her stomach returned.

"When this is over, you'll be dead," she whispered at the great white's receding figure.

TUNA
RUN

CHAPTER 30

GRAY WAS EXHAUSTED. THEY'D BEEN SWIMMING nonstop for days, eating only when they could do so while moving. Striiker led them toward the deepest of the Big Blue. With every tail stroke, Rogue Shiver moved closer to the middle of the North Atlantis and the Atlantis Spine, the undersea mountain range the bluefin followed for the Tuna Run. Gray and Barkley hoped it would lead them to their families and friends from the reef. But as important as finding their loved ones was, they knew that Velenka's plan must be stopped. If it wasn't, no one would be safe.

"You know," Barkley gasped through labored breaths, "It won't do any good if we go belly up before we get there!"

"It's just ahead!" Striiker shouted through the current. "Toughen up!"

Barkley grumbled but kept swimming. Gray sped up

so he could get a better look. He bumped into Striiker's tail when he saw the range.

Snork gave out a squeak and even Mari said, "Whoa." Everyone else was shocked into silence.

Gray had heard that in the landshark world there were huge mountains that stretched into the sky, much larger than any by the Caribbi reef where he was born. But they couldn't be larger than these! The immense, jagged mountain range rose from the Dark Blue as though it were the ocean's spine. Its depths were said to be deeper than any shark could swim and inhabited by monsters. Gray always thought those stories were something to scare pups, but seeing the blackness below, he shivered.

"So Striiker, you've been here," Mari began.

"Twice!" added Striiker.

The thresher rolled her eyes. "Right. So what happens? Tell us what to expect."

"The shivers take up positions either by the edge of the mountainside or away from it on the water side. I like the water side because you can be swept away if the tuna swerve too near to the rockside depending on if a legion or siege comes through. It's best to hunt from above or below the main body. If you get too deep inside the run you'll be battered. These dummies may be smaller than us, but get hit by a few hundred, and you'll swim the Sparkle Blue." Indeed, Gray could see most of the shivers that were already here set up to feed a good distance away from the jagged walls of the rockside. There were a good number of smaller shivers that couldn't get a good spot, though. Once again, Gray saw how it was an advantage to be the strongest shiver.

Barkley was becoming more nervous by the minute. "Good tip," he said as his voice cracked. "Don't get killed by our dinner."

Suddenly a swarming mass of bluefin swept through the area. Snork cried, "Look! We're missing it!"

"That's a shimmer at best," Striiker told the sawfish. Gray hid his embarrassment. He had almost launched himself toward the tuna but now saw the great white's count was accurate. "These are the shimmers and shoals that swim in front of the main Run. You can feed on them if you like, but most wait. It's tradition."

Barkley wasn't in favor of this. "Forget that," he said. "Let's feed now and stop Goblin's plan on a full stomach."

"You don't want to fight with a full stomach," Shell said. "Slows you down."

This made the dogfish sick with worry. "Oh, right," he answered in a quiet voice.

"If what you say is true, why's Razor Shiver on the rockside?" Mari asked.

"Because even though it is rockside, that particular spot is the best spot there is!" Striiker told the thresher and everyone else. "See how they're protected by the wall behind them?" Gray took note of the bulls in front of a jutting outcropping rearing from the mountainside. This formed an area where the current would be slower and they'd be protected as the tuna would undoubtedly swing wide to avoid running into the cliff wall. This way they could hunt the inner edge at their leisure. Tuna were dumb fish, but not even they were dumb enough to swim straight into the mountain.

"There's Goblin!" Shell said, pointing a fin. "Hmm, I was here last year with Razor, and they didn't set up there."

Striiker also looked perplexed. "Yeah, that's not their spot at all. They take the best water-side spot. That's not even a good spot. The current is really strong near the spine."

Gray couldn't figure out why Goblin would want to be on the rockside wall in front of the bulls. It seemed dangerous. Another shimmer, maybe even a double shimmer, roared through. A few sharks did catch a straggler or two, but not many.

Mari was trying to figure it out, too. "Striiker, what would happen if Razor and his shiver came out from that area protected by the wall?"

"They would never do that," he told her. "You'd take the brunt of the Run right in the face."

"But what if they were *pushed*?" she asked.

The bull shook its head at Mari. "Nah, it's very defensible," Shell said. "Razor's pretty smart. The shiver feeds in shifts, and there's always a group of sharks guarding their tails that would outnumber two to one anything Goblin could use to attack. If they tried anything from where they're set now, Goblin Shiver would get shoved into the Run because of the current and Razor Shiver."

Barkley swam in a quick circle. "Unless they were betrayed by bulls in their own shiver! That's it!" The dogfish explained: "Kilo and his fins will join Goblin Shiver while Razor and his Line are feeding! What Goblin doesn't know is that he's on the menu, too!"

"Kilo!" Shell growled the name. "I never liked that flipper. Too bad the giant clam didn't snap his face just a little tighter. Left a nice mark, though."

"WHAT?" Gray yelled so loudly Shell started.

The bull was taken aback. "Umm, when Kilo was a pup, he almost got eaten by a giant clam. The thing clamped onto his face—what does this have to do with anything?"

"Did it leave a scar like a clam shell?" Barkley asked, almost as wound up as Gray.

"Yeah," the bull said. "It sure did."

It all came together in Gray's mind. Barkley knew too, but neither could speak they were so overcome by emotion.

Finally the dogfish looked at him and said, "Tyro's tail. She's evil." Gray couldn't have agreed more.

Mari told the rest of the group, "Kilo led the bulls who destroyed their reef."

"So it wasn't Razor who ordered that. It was Goblin

and Velenka, after they learned about Coral Shiver's reef from Thrash!" said Barkley bitterly.

Gray could feel himself trembling with fury. All this time Goblin had stoked Gray's rage against Razor Shiver, when he was the one who had caused everything!

Barkley was angry but controlled it. "Gray, we're not here for revenge—"

"Speak for yourself!"

The dogfish bumped Gray hard in the flank. "You're not an evil shark!"

"Oh, come on, Barkley," said an exasperated Striiker. "If anyone deserves to swim the Sparkle Blue, it's Goblin!"

"I'm afraid I agree," Mari added.

Barkley shook his snout side-to-side "No! All we'll do is get ourselves killed. How does that help anything?" This gave everyone pause.

"Whatever you decide, I'll help," Snork said in a squeaky voice. "Or, I'll try my best. But how can we beat them all?"

"We don't have to," Barkley told him. "We can hurt Goblin *and* Velenka. It'll be worse than sending them to the Sparkle Blue."

"And how do we do that?" asked Shell.

"By spoiling their plans," Barkley answered with a grim smile. "By spoiling their plans."

Just then, a long, soulful whale call pierced the water around them. Then another and another! A thin, dense stream of bluefin tuna spilled into view. It was the Tuna Run! The fish were blue on top with silvered bellies that caught the sun rays and caused a million flashes of light, resembling the landshark fireworks Gray and Barkley once saw near the reef. They were so fast! Maybe not as fast as the speedy, speedy wahoo, but the difference wasn't enough to bet your life on. Their torpedo-shaped bodies shot through the water as their crescent tails churned, moving them faster and faster as they mindlessly swam to who knew where. The tuna Gray had caught on hunting trips by the reef were half this size. These were open-ocean bluefin, twice as long as the wahoo, weighing four and five times as much!

The dogfish spoke for everyone when he said, "Wow."

"It's beginning," Striiker told everyone. "If we get caught in the middle when the main mass comes through we won't make it to the other side."

Even now the stream of fish was getting thicker and more dense. "Then let's go," Gray shouted. The noise of bluefin tails churning caused a constant buzz even from this distance.

So Rogue Shiver swam into the Tuna Run to do battle and meet their destiny.

CHAPTER 31

"PEEL AWAY WHEN YOU'RE OVER RAZOR SHIVER!" Striiker yelled. "Don't get turned around and definitely don't get pushed inward! If we do that we can surprise Goblin!"

"And Kilo," muttered Gray darkly as he increased the pace of his tail strokes. The shark who had destroyed Gray's home finally had a name. The current was fast and made even more deadly by the bluefin who tore through the water as if they had been ordered to do so. Many shivers whizzed by, arrayed in loose groups, now readying to feed. There were so many!

One particular group caught Gray's eye. They weren't creeping up to feed like the others. They hovered in a perfect formation of three precisely stacked rows. And they were all marked. *Tattooed*, if Gray remembered the word correctly. What were sharks from Indi Shiver doing here?

Gray's thoughts were interrupted by a panicked Snork shouting, "I think we need to go faster!" as he struggled to keep up. The sawfish wasn't built for speed, swimming and hunting near the seabed where his long nose was an asset. If they went any faster, they would lose him entirely. They'd need everyone before this was over, though. Gray turned to see what had him so spooked.

Oh, no!

The main body of the Tuna Run rushed toward them like an undersea tidal wave of fish! It was a siege. At least! Maybe a double siege!

"Must swim faster! Everyone must swim faster!" shouted Barkley as he pushed Snork from behind.

Gray quickened his pace and swam for his life. The rock face to his right faded into a blur with glowing patches of distorted light from lumo clusters whizzing by at a terrifying pace. But they still weren't fast enough! The siege engulfed them, and everyone was battered from side to side. If they hadn't been swimming with the current, they would have undoubtedly been swept away to the Sparkle Blue.

"Go straight! Don't turn!" he heard Mari shout. She was only a body length away from him, but Gray couldn't see her at all, so thick were the bluefin. Then Gray saw another tattooed shark. But it wasn't someone from Indi Shiver.

It was Onyx! Gray hadn't put two and two together until this moment, but those really cool markings on Onyx were *Indi Shiver tattoos*!

And next to Onyx was Gray's mother! "Mom!" he shouted. "MOM!" He peeled off from the group.

"Are you crazy?!" shouted Striiker.

Finn yelled, "Gray, what are you doing?"

He took a look to see if Barkley was following, but the dogfish wasn't there.

His mother saw Gray and flicked her tail in a motion that indicated for him to stay away. She shouted, "It's too dangerous!"

Gray kept himself flowing with the tuna but was getting thumped more and more, glancing blows that threatened to turn him over. "WHERE CAN I FIND YOU?" he shouted. His mom answered, but Gray couldn't hear. There were too many bluefin whizzing by. "WHERE?" he shouted again as he was driven farther away by the mass of fish. Finally, Gray couldn't hold out and was pushed away from his mother. "I WILL FIND YOU!" he shouted. "I WILL FIND YOU!"

Then Gray was past them in an instant. She might have heard him. Were there others from the reef? Was that Quickeyes next to her? Gray was so focused on his mother he didn't know. But she was alive! His mother was alive! There was no going back, no fighting the siege while in the thick of it. Now, even glancing backward might get him killed. Gray would find her later, but there were things that needed to be done first. Besides, he couldn't have stopped if he wanted to.

Gray covered the distance left between himself and Razor Shiver in an eel strike. It took all his strength to muscle his way from the grip of the current and the running siege. He hoped the others had done the same.

Earlier, Gray held visions of skidding to a stop on a clam shell in front of Goblin, revealing his evil plan, and looking good doing it. That wasn't going to happen. As he forced his way sideways toward the rock face, he was rammed in the flank by a massive bluefin. Boom! Boom! Boom! Gray was smashed by three more and flipped over. Soon four- and five-hundred-pound fish were buffeting him from every angle. It was like being caught in the turbulence of a tidal wave and forced through a maze of coral, but a hundred times worse. Somehow Gray was ejected from the mass. He hit the wall sideways above Razor Shiver. Shell was already there, shaking his head, dazed.

"You all right?" Gray yelled over the noise of the siege. Luckily both of them were only bruised. The bull waggled his fins, indicating he was okay. As Gray got his fins working again, he saw that Striiker and Mari were much farther away, too distant to join with them for a while. They'd have to fight their way against the current to where he and Shell were. Gray looked for Barkley and Snork, but there was no sign of either. If they were gone there would be time to grieve later. The coup was happening now!

Razor and his shiver sharks hunted the edge of the Run as it continued roaring past. But he didn't see Kilo and ten other bulls swim into an attack formation with Goblin, and twenty other sharkkind. Razor and his Line would be shoved into the Tuna Run and never seen again!

It was all happening so fast! Gray needed to do something right now! He pumped his tail ferociously, fighting the current, but couldn't reach Goblin in time to stop the attack. The great white bore down on Razor and the bull didn't see him.

Just then, by skill or crazy luck—probably crazy luck—Barkley shot out of the siege of bluefin. He was spinning with tremendous speed and hit Thrash, who then knocked into Goblin, Streak, and Ripper, sending them all plunging beyond Razor. Even though it was only a short distance, it was strategically huge because now they needed to fight the current to regain position.

But before Goblin could get back into position to attack, Razor saw him swimming with Kilo and other sharks from his shiver. He understood instantly, and shouted, "Traitors!"

Every bull with Razor—easily forty—charged the outnumbered Goblin Shiver and the disloyal bulls. It was chaos! Razor swam at the head of his phalanx of sharks in a tight formation. They let themselves be carried toward Goblin and his allies, who barely avoided being swept away. The two shivers met near the edge of the safe area by the rock wall with a crash loud enough to be heard over the roar of the bluefin—and now Gray and Shell were in the middle of the battle!

"You!" shouted Goblin when he saw Gray. Anger and hate shined in his eyes. The big great white would have gone straight for him if there weren't so many bulls streaking in every direction. Gray swam away from Goblin Shiver, avoiding raking attacks from Streak and another shiver shark, a thresher. Shell and Gray were then spotted by Razor. Razor thought they, too, were with Goblin!

Gray and Shell fought their way through Razor Shiver while staying in front of Goblin and his forces. They swam full-speed ahead, flank to flank, so tightly an urchin spine couldn't have fit between them. Everything was flashing teeth, blood, confusion, and above all, the thunderous din of the bluefin siege flashing by, a relentless, speeding, silvery mass. Gray didn't want to kill anyone, but he defended himself fiercely. He butted two attacking bulls off the safe area, and both were sucked into the Run as if jerked away by a giant octopus tentacle.

While Gray and Shell were handling anything coming snout to snout, swimming fast enough to keep Goblin Shiver from biting their tails, neither was defended from above.

That's exactly where Velenka and three others attacked from.

They streaked downward, and there was nothing Gray or Shell could do. If they stopped churning forward, Goblin Shiver would catch them. If they stopped defending from the bulls attacking head-on, they were also done.

"Get away from them!" came a shout.

It was Mari! And Striiker! They had fought the current and bluefin to make it back when it mattered most. Mari would have taken Velenka's dorsal if she hadn't peeled off her attack, which saved Gray. Striiker smashed into Shell's pursuer, biting him in the gills and forcing the dying shark into the current. All of the attackers were swept away by the Tuna Run. Now Gray, Shell, Striiker, and Mari were up current from both shivers, which were busy fighting with each other.

"What took you so long?" Gray shouted to Striiker and Mari over the noise of the swimming tuna.

"Just doing a little sightseeing," the great white replied with a grin.

Everyone was catching their breath when Snork made his appearance. He was scratched and bruised, but otherwise okay. "Sorry I'm late," he told everyone.

But where was Barkley?

The area cleared as the siege moved itself farther away from the rock face. Gray could now see the battle clearly. Both shivers lost many sharks, but Razor's fins still outnumbered Goblin's. Razor's first said something to him and the bull leader nodded. He yelled, "I'll deal with you all later!" Razor and his shiver caught the current and disappeared with the thinning bluefin.

They had done it! They'd stopped Goblin and Velenka's plan!

This triumphant feeling was short-lived as Gray saw their situation. The Tuna Run tapered to a thin flow of stragglers and older fish. The current also lessened, as it had been partly driven by the bluefin themselves, and there weren't so many now. Goblin and his forces formed a massive attack formation. There were at least twenty-five Goblin Shiver sharkkind in three levels along with the remaining bulls.

Velenka stared at Gray and the others hatefully. "Kill them, Goblin! Eat them alive!"

As if Goblin needed any goading. There was no way the five sharks of Rogue Shiver could win this fight. Shell and Striiker were too injured to swim away. Snork wasn't fast enough. And Gray wouldn't leave his friends behind.

Not now, or ever again.

At least Goblin and his shiver sharks were slowed by their own injuries. It wouldn't help for long, but it didn't allow Goblin and his force to charge right away. "What are you waiting for?" cried Velenka from a distance.

Goblin panted for a moment, but that was all the time his hate would allow him to rest. "ATTACK!" he cried and rushed Gray and his friends, intent on eating them all.

But Goblin Shiver was exhausted from the fight with Razor. Struggling against even the weakened current, they seemed as if they were swimming in slow motion. Gray got in front of Mari, while Striiker and Shell swam to either side of Gray to protect his flanks. It looked like Snork was running away, but instead he made a vertical half loop and took position hovering topside. Gray was so proud of his friends. But he suspected that their formation wouldn't last more than a few seconds after the battle began.

"I see you've found better fins to call friends!" said Takiza, hovering next to Gray's left eye.

"I guess so." If Gray had had any strength left at all, he would have been more surprised to see Takiza. But he was too tired to be surprised. The betta didn't seem to be affected by the currents whipsawing around them. His frilly fins waved gently as if he was in a much calmer ocean. "How have you been, otherwise?"

Gray was utterly worn out and sure he'd heard Takiza wrong. "You may want to leave now!" he yelled over the dull roar of the bluefin passing. "Goblin wants to eat us!"

"No. We have much to discuss," said the colorful betta. "I'd like you to become my apprentice! Do you agree?"

Gray blinked at the smiling betta. The frilly fish was mad! "Fine," Gray told him. "If we live through this, I'll be your apprentice."

"Excellent!"

The appearance of the betta caused Goblin to slow down. It seemed he feared the tiny, ruffled fish. "This has nothing to do with you, Takiza!" the great white growled.

"You have the manners of a lumpfish and the odor of sea kelp baking in the sun," the betta told him. "Go now or I will become annoyed!"

Striiker's eyes popped open. "Who's this, now?"

"Shh!" Shell hissed.

Mari agreed. "Yeah, I wanna see this."

Goblin didn't take it well, that's for sure. "You'll grow annoyed? You—*you*? Will . . . be . . . *annoyed*?!" he sputtered. "I'll show you annoy—"

That's as far as the great white got.

Takiza fluttered his frilly fins and did a slow barrel roll, and a whirling mass of glowing water grew in the middle of the Goblin Shiver, sucking them inside while it expanded. Velenka was so shocked that she just stared at the betta as she was pulled into it, not swimming against the force even a little.

Goblin did, though. And mightily.

It was impressive how the infuriated great white kept himself outside the whirling maelstrom for a while, even though his tail was caught. "This isn't over!" he shouted. Gray didn't know if he was talking to him or to Takiza, but was too tired to care. "This isn't over, I tell you!" Then Goblin was hauled into the roiling, shining, water ball.

The sharkkind inside were spinning at a tremendous speed. It wasn't hurting them, Gray saw, but they'd be dizzy for a week. With a flick of Takiza's tail, the ball moved into the current and was carried away into the distance. The betta snapped his frilly fins and the glowing ball disappeared. Goblin and everyone else tumbled away with the current.

Takiza passed Striiker, Mari, Shell, and Snork, giving them all polite nods. Nobody returned the greeting, mainly because they were so awed and dumbfounded. The siamese fighting fish stopped in front of Gray to say, "I'll tell you when your training is to begin. Until then, I bid you good day." And with that Takiza Jaelynn Betta vam Delacrest Waveland ka Boom Boom swam away, humming a sprightly tune.

"Seriously, who is that?" asked Snork.

Just then, Barkley appeared. Gray's heart leapt when he saw his friend. The dogfish had a giant lump on his head and was swimming at an angle.

"What happened?" he asked. "Did I miss anything?"

Everyone hooted with laughter. Barkley looked at them, perplexed. "What?" he asked, which made everyone laugh even harder.

CHAPTER 32

BECAUSE OF HIS SIZE, GRAY COULD NO LONGER use the crack in the hull of the tri-level landshark wreck to get inside, so his friends widened a back entrance that was rotting away.

"Don't take this question as an insult," Barkley said after they were inside, "but how much more do you think you're going to grow?"

"And less fatty fish taste almost as good as the, umm, fatty ones," Mari added.

"Not really," Shell said.

"Yeah, about that," Gray began. "I don't know how much bigger I'll get, because I'm not a reef shark."

"What do you mean?" asked Striiker. "You said you were."

"Because that's what I thought. I'm actually . . . I might be . . . wow, this sounds crazy—"

Barkley slapped him on the flank with his tail. "Spit it out!"

"I'm a megalodon."

There was silence. They all just stared at him. "Velenka took me into the prehistore cave, where there was this skeleton. . . . My teeth matched . . . and, uh, I actually kinda look like it."

"That's so cool!" said Snork. "I thought all megalodons were extinct, though."

"They are extinct!" said Striiker. "But I've been to that cave, and I gotta say there is a resemblance. Gray is definitely as ugly as that thing." The great white gave him a good-natured smile. "Maybe even uglier!"

Mari swam close, looking into his mouth. "Open," she instructed, and he did. Pretty soon everyone was crowding around for a better look. "Wider!" Now Gray couldn't close his mouth because Mari's snout was actually in there.

"His teeth do match. They're smaller, but they're the same curved shape," the thresher told everyone. "I love the prehistore cave. I've been in there twenty times."

"By the way, you have a bluefin head stuck in your back row," Snork told him.

"Even if him being a megalodon is true," Shell began, "how *can* it be true?"

"Umm, hahh-loww?" Gray said as best he could while the others held a conversation practically *inside* of his mouth. "Could ya pluhs back awahhhh?" They did, and he closed his mouth. "Private space, anyone?"

Barkley was the only one who hadn't said anything. Gray could see the look on his face. He got that expression when he was thinking hard about something. Then the dogfish nodded to himself and broke his silence. "This makes sense. It really does."

"Please, enlighten us," Striiker said sarcastically.

"Velenka knew it. Knew it right away, somehow," Barkley explained. "She wanted Gray all along. She pulled the strings to get Goblin to find the reef, to make sure we were homeless, everything."

"So Velenka's smart," the sawfish said, "but in a really bad way."

"That's exactly right, Snork. And Gray," the dogfish said evenly, "I don't think she's done with you."

"Neither is Goblin," Striiker added quietly.

"Then I'll leave. It'll be safer for all of you."

"No, Gray," Mari said. "Striiker means Goblin isn't done with any of us. Neither is Razor, for that matter." Gray looked over at the great white, and he nodded, agreeing with the thresher.

"Another one of your jelly-brained ideas," Barkley said with a chuckle. "But we have a better plan."

Striiker moved to the front of the pack. "You should lead us."

"No," Gray said. "This is your shiver. I couldn't."

"You can and you will. What you did at the Tuna Run

showed me how much I have to learn about being a real leader."

Gray looked at Barkley, Mari, Shell, and Snork. They were all in on it. Gray was touched. He'd told them he was a megalodon and they didn't think he was a monster. They still wanted him as their friend. And they trusted him to lead them.

"Would you be my first?" Gray asked the great white. Striiker grinned.

"Can you two fight or yell at each other now?" Barkley asked. "I liked it better when you were fighting." This brought out a round of good-natured laughter—something they all needed.

Rogue Shiver was reborn! There were many problems, to be sure, but for some reason Gray felt hopeful.

"Group rub!" Snork shouted. Soon they were all yelling, laughing, and scraping against each other. It was a great ending to an absolutely terrifying day. But not perfect. On the way back from the Tuna Run, Barkley and Gray had talked. Neither had seen any sign of his mother or anyone else from Coral Shiver.

Or Indi Shiver, which also bothered Gray for some nagging reason. And what was Onyx's connection to a shiver from another ocean? That was a question to be answered later. For now they could take comfort in the fact that Coral Shiver was alive. They were out there somewhere. Gray would never stop searching until he found them. Barkley and the rest of his new friends would help. All in all, it was the best Gray could hope for right now. Tomorrow was another day to find the answers he was looking for. And his mom.

No one noticed Takiza smile and swim away from the greenie-covered porthole.

EPILOGUE

VELENKA STILL COULDN'T BELIEVE WHAT HAD happened. The little betta had tossed the combined might of Goblin Shiver aside with no effort at all. She'd heard stories when she was a pup about the magical fighting fish but had never believed them. All her carefully laid plans had been swept aside by his frilly fins! How could she harness Takiza's power for her own desires? How indeed?

"We will find them," Goblin growled while hovering over Speakers Rock. "We'll defeat all our enemies!" The ceremony to make Kilo his third was over. Velenka thought that elevating the bull into the Line wasn't a good idea, especially after Kilo's efforts brought nothing. But Velenka couldn't talk Goblin into anything right now. As it was, Streak wasn't pleased by being passed over by a traitor, and Ripper didn't like the ex-Razor Shiver bull, either.

At least she was able to soothe Thrash's bruised ego. She stepped aside, rather than fighting him for fourth in the Line. Not that she thought she could beat him in a fair fight, anyway. Goblin wasn't happy. He was in the mood for blood. The great white would be even less pleased if he found out that Velenka had *told* Thrash to challenge her, and that she wouldn't stand in his way.

"They won't leave the Atlantis. I can feel it. And when we find them, there will be blood!" Goblin roared to the approval of the gathered shiver sharks.

But whose? Velenka thought silently as she nodded and gnashed her teeth in support. Was tiny Rogue Shiver under the protection of Takiza? And even if it wasn't, Gray was a megalodon. That was a definite problem. He needed to be converted to her cause or killed before he got too powerful. She would have to think carefully about her next move.

"Who will swim by my flank and send the traitors to the Sparkle Blue?" yelled Goblin to the shiver. Everyone answered with a rousing roar.

Velenka made sure she cheered the loudest.

EJ ALTBACKER is a screenwriter who has worked on television shows including *Green Lantern: The Animated Series*, *Ben 10*, *Mucha Lucha*, and *Spider-Man*. He lives in Hermosa Beach, California. *Shark Wars* is his first book.